An Ecstasy Romance™

"YOU GIVE YOURSELF TO OTHER MEN, ONE MORE CAN'T MAKE ANY DIFFERENCE."

The insulting words tore through JoAnna as if they had been shards of glass. Her entire body stiffened from the wound.

"Let go of me!" she cried, anger and hurt lending strength to her renewed struggles against the tightness of his hold.

Slowly Luke released her, his pale eyes icy and hard, his lips a thin line of displeasure as he fought to master his surging emotions.

"All right . . . you win. This time. But I promise you one thing, JoAnna Davis. One day you won't be begging for me to set you free."

CANDLELIGHT ECSTASY ROMANCES™

1. THE TAWNY GOLD MAN, *Amii Lorin*
2. GENTLE PIRATE, *Jayne Castle*
3. THE PASSIONATE TOUCH, *Bonnie Drake*
4. THE SHADOWED REUNION, *Lillian Cheatham*
5. ONLY THE PRESENT, *Noelle Berry McCue*
6. LEAVES OF FIRE, FLAME OF LOVE, *Susan Chatfield*
7. THE GAME IS PLAYED, *Amii Lorin*
8. OCEAN OF REGRETS, *Noelle Berry McCue*
9. SURRENDER BY MOONLIGHT, *Bonnie Drake*
10. GENTLEMAN IN PARADISE, *Harper McBride*
11. MORGAN WADE'S WOMAN, *Amii Lorin*
12. THE TEMPESTUOUS LOVERS, *Suzanne Simmons*
13. THE MARRIAGE SEASON, *Sally Dubois*
14. THE HEART'S AWAKENING, *Valerie Ferris*
15. DESPERATE LONGINGS, *Frances Flores*
16. BESIEGED BY LOVE, *Maryann Young*
17. WAGERED WEEKEND, *Jayne Castle*
18. SWEET EMBER, *Bonnie Drake*
19. TENDER YEARNINGS, *Elaine Raco Chase*
20. THE FACE OF LOVE, *Anne N. Reisser*
21. LOVE'S ENCORE, *Rachel Ryan*
22. BREEZE OFF THE OCEAN, *Amii Lorin*
23. RIGHT OF POSSESSION, *Jayne Castle*
24. THE CAPTIVE LOVE, *Anne N. Reisser*
25. FREEDOM TO LOVE, *Sabrina Myles*
26. BARGAIN WITH THE DEVIL, *Jayne Castle*
27. GOLDEN FIRE, SILVER ICE, *Marisa de Zavala*
28. STAGES OF LOVE, *Beverly Sommers*
29. LOVE BEYOND REASON, *Rachel Ryan*
30. PROMISES TO KEEP, *Rose Marie Ferris*
31. WEB OF DESIRE, *Jean Hager*
32. SENSUOUS BURGUNDY, *Bonnie Drake*
33. DECEPTIVE LOVE, *Anne N. Reisser*
34. STOLEN HOLIDAY, *Marjorie Eatock*
35. THAT ISLAND, THAT SUMMER, *Belle Thorne*
36. A MAN'S PROTECTION, *Jayne Castle*
37. AFTER THE FIRE, *Rose Marie Ferris*

CALL IT LOVE

Ginger Chambers

A CANDLELIGHT ECSTASY ROMANCE™

Published by
Dell Publishing Co., Inc.
1 Dag Hammarskjold Plaza
New York, New York 10017

*For Steve—my best friend,
my husband, my love. . . .*

Copyright © 1982 by Ginger Chambers

All rights reserved. No part of this book may be
reproduced or transmitted in any form or by any
means, electronic or mechanical, including photocopying,
recording or by any information storage
and retrieval system, without the written permission
of the Publisher, except where permitted by law.

Dell ® TM 681510, Dell Publishing Co., Inc.

Candlelight Ecstasy Romance™ is a trademark of
Dell Publishing Co., Inc., New York, New York.

ISBN: 0-440-11128-5

Printed in the United States of America

First printing—February 1982

Dear Reader:

In response to your enthusiasm for Candlelight Ecstasy Romances™, we are now increasing the number of titles per month from three to four.

We are pleased to offer you sensuous novels set in America, depicting modern American women and men as they confront the provocative problems of a modern relationship.

Throughout the history of the Candlelight line, Dell has tried to maintain a high standard of excellence, to give you the finest in reading pleasure. It is now and will remain our most ardent ambition.

Editor
Candlelight Romances

CHAPTER ONE

The slender figure of a girl moved gracefully along the edge of the water, hands pushed deeply into the front pockets of her jeans, bare toes abstractedly scuffing the surface of the sand. The ever-present breeze from the Gulf of Mexico playfully ruffled her short honey-blond curls while the hot Texas sun blazed down in typical July fashion. Close by several low-flying gulls swooped and gave their strident cry; but the girl ignored them, just as she ignored the voice that called from a distance.

"JoAnna! Wait! Please!"

JoAnna kept walking, her delicate features set in stiff lines.

"You've got to listen to me, JoAnna! You don't understand!"

The girl didn't pause; the only sign of her having heard was the further tightening of her soft lips.

Soon heavy footfalls thudded on the damp sand behind her and hard fingers reached out to bite into the tender flesh of her upper arm, turning her about abruptly.

JoAnna tensed, a deep burning anger glowing in the depths of her brilliant green eyes as she lifted them to face the man who had stopped her. "Just what am I not supposed to understand, Philip?" she demanded. "How you used me?" With one disgusted jerk her arm was free.

She started to turn away but the man took a step forward, blocking her movement. His breath was still short from his run and his usually perfectly styled dark hair was in disorder.

"It's not like you think, JoAnna! Not at all! You've *got* to let me explain! I'm getting a divorce. As soon as it's humanly possible, I'm getting a divorce!"

Almond-shaped emerald eyes rejected the classical good looks of the man standing so close to her. Melissa had been right all along, she thought grimly. She had tried to warn her about trusting a man like Philip Cole. But at the time her infatuation had been so great that she had not wanted to listen. Philip had come into her well-ordered life and turned it upside down. For months she had wandered around in a daze—until this morning, that was.

"Now that *is* an interesting bit of news," she jeered. "And since *I* know, why don't you try telling your wife! Oh, but remember to do it carefully. It may come as quite a shock . . . her being pregnant and all."

"She told you *that?*" Philip looked like a man who had been hit, hard, in the stomach.

"Along with a few other things," JoAnna confirmed coldly. In a gesture of mingled contempt and dismissal, she turned her back and started to walk away.

Philip lunged forward, once again impeding her progress. "I won't let you do this, JoAnna!"

"You don't have a choice, Philip! All along you lied to me. You told me you were already divorced—that you had been for the past year. And I believed you!"

"I lied because I knew you wouldn't have anything to do with me if I didn't! Alice and I were as good as divorced. There was nothing left of our marriage! We were like two strangers!"

"Two *strangers* don't have babies, Philip! Or are you trying to tell me that the child isn't yours?"

Philip's dark eyes could not leave the smoldering anger of her own. Finally he choked out, "No, it's mine—but Alice tricked me! She knew I was seeing someone else and she's spiteful enough not to want to let me be happy!"

Several long seconds passed before JoAnna questioned softly, "What happened? Did she rape you?"

The man winced visibly under her taunting. Then a look of desperation settled on his chiseled features and his hands shot out to pull her tightly against his body.

"I don't want to lose you, JoAnna—I can't lose you! I love you!"

Instinctively JoAnna tried to push away. "You don't know what love *is,* Philip!"

"I know that I don't want to live without you!" he rasped thickly.

A harsh laugh escaped JoAnna's lips. "Oh, I think you'll manage to survive. From what Alice told me, you've had yourself quite a time since you married her— one affair after another." She caught her breath sharply. "Do you have any idea of how I felt with her sitting there, telling me so sweetly and with such understanding that I was only one in a *line!* " Tears of remembered humiliation flooded JoAnna's eyes and she lowered her chin quickly, not wanting Philip to see.

But Philip did see and was quick to take advantage of her seeming weakness. He put his mouth close to her ear and whispered urgently, "But you're different, JoAnna. Okay, yes," he rushed on when he felt her stiffen. "I admit it. There have been others. But with you it *is* different! I love you and I want you—you almost drive me insane with wanting you!" He buried his mouth against her neck, his lips moving along the sensitive skin as he breathed achingly. "I want you now."

JoAnna tried again to free herself, the degree of revulsion she was experiencing from his attempt at lovemaking shaking her. How could she have ever thought she loved this man? She must have been temporarily insane! But her struggles did no good. Uncaring of the hurt he inflicted, Philip used his superior strength to counteract her every move. When finally he raised his head, his dark eyes were glistening with arrogant confidence, as if sure his brand of persuasion would prove effective in the end.

JoAnna stared up at him, seeing him clearly for the first time. He was an extremely handsome man: His hair so dark and smoothly textured it looked like black mink, his thin patrician features almost too perfect, he had a charm so practiced and easy that he was hard to resist. Yes, he had everything—all the attributes a woman could want in a man. All except truth, fidelity, honor.... Suddenly her stomach lurched and she had to swallow hard before she could speak.

"What you don't seem to understand, Philip, is that *I* don't want *you*."

An ugly expression settled over Philip's features as he saw the depth of her determination. "That's not what you said last night," he reminded her roughly.

JoAnna firmed her chin. "Last night was last night. Things change."

"Not that much they don't! Last night you wanted me—you wanted me so badly you almost let me take you. And for a woman like you, that has to mean something!" There was a nasty edge to his voice.

"No!" JoAnna denied, not wanting to be reminded.

"I can make you feel that way again, JoAnna." He pretended not to hear her. "Let me make you feel that way again." His arms tightened with purpose as he lowered his head.

JoAnna began to struggle in earnest, twisting, turning, making it hard for him to contain her, deflecting the touch of his lips. But her continued resistance only served to infuriate Philip, and he shook her with some force.

"I'll get a divorce, I tell you! I'll even marry you if I have to!"

JoAnna couldn't help the peal of laughter that escaped her. It was a high, mocking sound that grated even on her ears. "My, you *are* getting desperate," she taunted.

Philip swore viciously. "I'll make you love me!"

Repugnance burned in JoAnna's expressive eyes as she spat, "Go to hell, Philip!"

A tremor shuddered through the man's long form and his mouth tightened into a thin, ugly line. "You little bitch," he rasped softly. "You tormenting, desirable little bitch." Roughly he jerked her forward, his lips fastening onto hers, grinding her tender skin against her teeth until she tasted the salty tang of blood.

Philip's breathing was ragged when finally he lifted his head, and his dark eyes glittered with aroused desire. "I've wanted you for too long to let you go now. I've held back more with you than I have any woman, waiting for you to make up your mind. But I'm not waiting any longer! At least I'm going to get something out of the months I've wasted!"

He plucked her from the sand and began to walk away, carrying her. JoAnna fought him with all her strength, but as before, it did no good.

"Put me down, Philip!" she cried, for the first time experiencing fear. Philip paid her no mind, making his way up the beach and only stopping when close to the sheltering sanddunes with their tall needlelike grass. "Put me down—now!" she commanded, but her voice broke on the last word.

Philip's laugh was disdainful. "All right, my sweet, I will!" He lowered her onto the soft sand and stretched out beside her, all in one fluid motion.

JoAnna attempted to roll away as soon as she felt the first grains of sand beneath her but Philip stopped her escape with the weight of his body. Frantically she turned her face away from his hot, moist kisses, rejecting what only yesterday she had found desirable. She uttered a cry of both outrage and fear as the material of her old cotton shirt was torn open, leaving the creamy, rounded swells of her breasts exposed to his view.

"God, but you're beautiful," he whispered roughly, bending to devour hungrily the rosy-tipped peaks. JoAnna fought with increasing fervor, the intimate touch of his lips abhorrent to her.

Then he was sitting astride her, the strong muscles of his legs holding her straining body as effectively as his one hand held her arms above her head. A primitive whimper of terror passed JoAnna's lips as she saw him reach down to pull at the snap to her jeans.

"No, Philip! *No!*" she cried, desperately working against the bruising pressure of the hand that was holding her wrists. If she could only pull at his hair or rake his face with her fingernails. . . . He was like a crazed demon! She had never suspected he could be so ruthless. And she had never known herself capable of the hatred she now felt for him. Love was akin to hate, she had once heard. Now she

12

knew it to be true. She wanted to bite, to scratch, to hurt. If she had a gun, she would use it. . . .

"Hold still, damn you!"

Philip was finding it difficult to loosen her jeans with only one hand free and her unyielding body inhibiting his every try. But his persistence was finally rewarded and the snap gave. The zipper followed immediately.

"I hate you—I hate you!" JoAnna cried over and over.

Just as Philip began to tug the jeans lower, a voice came from close beside them, making his hand freeze.

"I believe the lady has made her feelings known, don't you . . . friend?"

A dull red surged up Philip's neck as he raised his head slowly and stared blankly at the man standing so still not two feet away.

JoAnna turned wide green eyes to the stranger. Her first impression was of his size. From her prone position, he fairly towered over them. Next she became aware of hard, bronzed muscles—a broad expanse of muscular chest roughened by a liberal sprinkling of dark, curling hair and narrowing down to a flat, hard stomach. His taut, lean hips were encased in faded cut-off jeans and showed a long length of well-muscled legs above bare feet. To her dazed mind he looked exactly like some kind of avenging god who had been sent to earth with the express mission of rescuing her. If he had raised his hand and lightning had struck from a clear sky, she would have been unsurprised. But strangely, it was his quiet, almost deceptive air of calm that magnified the impression of tremendous power—a power that was momentarily being held in check. JoAnna swallowed convulsively.

The stranger's leashed violence must not have filtered

through to Philip's consciousness because he began to sputter. "Look here, this is none of your business—"

The hard voice interrupted cuttingly. "You *made* it my business, friend, when you decided to use my front yard for your fun and games." He gave a slight motion of his dark head toward the derelict beach house positioned directly behind them. It was a companion to JoAnna's own, but she had not known that it was occupied. For years it had sat unattended, wind and weather taking their toll.

Finally the precarious position he was in must have found its way through the fog in Philip's brain, because he released JoAnna and began to scuttle away, so resembling a sand crab that if she had not experienced such upset in the last few minutes, JoAnna would have laughed aloud. As it was she bit down on her abused bottom lip and tried to cover herself with the remnants of her torn blouse.

After a moment, the man's pale eyes came to rest on her—their smoky mixture of gray and blue a startling contrast to his tanned skin. "You want me to hold him for the police?" he asked, watching her steadily yet knowing exactly where Philip was, ready to spring toward him if need be.

JoAnna stared up at him, at the ruggedness of his features—at the high cheekbones, straight, masculine nose, and thinly drawn mouth that were too compelling, too strong to be termed merely handsome. She tore her eyes away to look at Philip, who was now sitting hunched over, his complexion a sickly shade of greenish gray. "No. Just . . . so long as he leaves," she whispered. She didn't want to see Philip again—ever.

The man transferred his gaze to Philip. "You heard what the lady said. Get going."

Philip's head jerked upward, hectic color rushing into

each cheek and standing out in two vivid spots. His dark eyes flashed with both shame and defiance but in the end his self-serving character won out. "She's no lady!" he spat out vindictively. "Far from it! Ask her how she's led me on . . . how she gets me to where I can't think any more and then changes her mind!" He turned his handsome face toward JoAnna, and it was so contorted with malevolence that she flinched. "Deep down you're a cold-hearted, selfish little bitch! And no man—no real man—is ever going to put up with you." He actually began to shake his finger at her, laying all the blame squarely on her shoulders, conveniently forgetting his own duplicity. "There's a name for women like you—"

The stranger took several quick steps forward until he was standing above Philip, who had swung about to watch his approach with all the fascination of a rabbit watching a snake. One large bronzed hand shot out to grip Philip's collar, pulling him off balance and almost bringing him to his knees.

"I think that's about enough out of you," the man breathed menacingly before thrusting the shaking Philip away. "Go on—clear out—before I change my mind and beat the hell out of you."

Without glancing again toward JoAnna, Philip stumbled away across the sand and back to the car he had left parked in her driveway.

The stranger watched him go, his lips a thin line and his jaw tight. When he glanced back around at JoAnna, he found her sitting up, one hand grasping the edges of her shirt together over her breasts and the other wiping away a tear that was spilling down over her cheek. She was trembling now, reaction setting in.

"Do you think you can walk?" The deep voice startled her.

"I—yes, I think so."

"Come on then." The stranger moved toward her and extended a hand to help her up. It was several long moments before JoAnna allowed herself to accept it. Men had never frightened her before—growing up with three older brothers had seen to that. But today her confidence had received a decided jolt.

Getting to her feet proved to be no problem, especially with the aid of the man's strong arm; staying there was. Her knees felt like so much Jell-o and were shaking so badly that they refused to support her weight. She swayed and was instantly scooped up to be held against a muscular chest that was as solid as rock. Only the warmth of his skin and the steady rise and fall of his breathing gave evidence that it was flesh.

Instinctively JoAnna stiffened. The man paused to look down at her, a smile momentarily softening the harshness of his features.

"Relax," he murmured. "I've never found it necessary to use force on a woman, and I certainly don't plan to start now."

JoAnna stared at him, at the pale eyes and dark mane of brown hair that waved slightly in the breeze. What he said could in no way be construed as a boast. Even shaken as she was, she could see that. With those hard, rugged features, lean, powerful body, and that air of danger combined with a disturbing brand of masculine sensuality—women probably made fools of themselves with boring regularity trying to gain the smallest measure of his attention.

JoAnna promptly dismissed the idea. She had had

enough of men and their desires for one day. What she wanted now was to go home and lick her wounds in private. Her day had started early for a Saturday—Alice Cole dragging her out of a sound sleep at seven thirty and talking almost nonstop for the next half hour. Then her showdown with Philip. . . . Her stomach dropped at the vision of what most certainly would have occurred if the stranger had not appeared.

He covered the distance to her beach house in no time, then the long flight of exterior stairs that led to the front verandah, her slight weight seeming to mean nothing to the man. The door was ajar so they moved unimpeded into the shaded coolness of the small living room. There the man hesitated, the sudden change from the outside brightness momentarily blinding him. Then he moved across the room to lower her onto the sofa.

"I think what you need is a drink. Got anything that would do?"

JoAnna motioned toward the kitchen cabinets that could be seen above the open breakfast bar. "I think there's something in there, but I don't—"

He moved away without waiting for her to finish. In the kitchen he made himself totally at home, going through her cabinets searching for what he wanted. When he returned, he held out a glass that contained an extra measure of a rich amber liquid.

"Here, drink this."

JoAnna did as she was told, the full strength of the liquor making her cough but the warmth of it coursing through her numbed limbs and making her feel stronger. As she finished the last sip, she felt his pale eyes searching her small face thoroughly. "Did he hurt you?" he asked finally.

JoAnna raised her eyes to meet the unfathomable expression in his.

"N-no—not really." Forcibly she stilled the trembling that once again set in at the reminder of what had almost happened. It would take more than a double neat whiskey to make her completely insensitive. Her green eyes darkened and she played with the glass that was still in her hand, unconsciously twisting it around and around. "I never thanked you for helping me." Her voice was low and husky.

The man shrugged the powerful muscles of his shoulders. "At first I wasn't sure that you needed help." At her puzzled look he explained, "Some women like to put up a fight just to heighten the enjoyment of the moment."

As the meaning of his words became clear, a deep flush rose up into JoAnna's cheeks. At twenty-five and in this day and age, she should be accustomed to blunt speech in sexual matters. But somehow, coming from this man, it only flustered her.

"Yes . . . well . . ." she stumbled; then, on seeing his slow smile, she looked away, her fingers automatically clutching tighter on the remaining fabric that was attempting to cover her breasts. Her embarrassment increased as she suddenly became aware of her state of near undress and she rose to her feet quickly. But to her dismay, as she did her loosened jeans started to slide down over her hips. With a startled gasp she made a grab for them; but by saving herself from one disaster, she created another. The remnants of her shirt fell apart and it was several long moments before she could jerk the material back together —enough time to afford the man standing across from her a rich display of her nakedness.

Her cheeks were a fiery red as she mumbled stiffly,

"I—I need to change." She was stating the obvious but could think of nothing else to say.

"Can you make it on your own?"

JoAnna nodded shortly. Right now her only wish was that he would go away! She appreciated the help he had given her, but they could further their acquaintance another time—if what he had said about living next door was true.

The man did not seem to share in her opinion because at that moment he was lowering his large frame into a chair and sitting back comfortably.

"I'll wait here," he decided.

"You don't have to," JoAnna replied a trifle desperately.

"No problem. I haven't anything else to do at the moment."

JoAnna sent him a harried look before scurrying from the room.

When she returned after throwing what was left of her shirt into a wicker trash basket and donning a fresh blouse, the man was still resting comfortably in the chair. His gaze flickered over her, watching her graceful movements as she crossed in front of him to resume her previous position on the sofa.

"You have a nice place here," he commented, his gaze moving around the room only to stop momentarily on the large collection of shells and driftwood that was spread out on a work table in front of the double windows facing the Gulf.

"Thank you." JoAnna's color was still not back to normal. Somehow the man unnerved her.

The silence between them lengthened. Finally JoAnna,

who had been fiddling with the fringe of a sofa pillow, broke it by asking, "I take it you're my new neighbor?"

"You take it right."

"Did you just move in?" Her laugh was a bit strained. "I mean, I haven't seen you around before."

"I moved in yesterday—if you could call it moving in. Just myself and a suitcase."

"Oh."

Silence settled between them again. But this time JoAnna was completely devoid of ideas to further their conversation. How much longer was he planning to stay? Surely he could see that she wanted to be by herself!

"Was he your boyfriend?"

JoAnna jumped at the sudden question. She shot a startled look at the man's bronzed face. He was watching her steadily.

"I—I thought he was."

"Under the circumstances, I don't think it would be a good idea for you to see him again."

JoAnna shuddered slightly at the understatement. "I won't," she assured him.

"He may not agree with that."

"He'll have to!"

The man's pale eyes narrowed and he spoke slowly, carefully. "From what I saw last night, he might have cause to think you're playing with him—and that maybe you didn't like it that I interfered today." JoAnna gasped but he went on as if unaware of the shock his words had dealt. "Do you always do your lovemaking on the beach?"

For a moment JoAnna sat in stunned amazement, then all the blood seemed to drain from her face. She couldn't believe what she had just heard. She looked at him as if he were a viper who had been biding his time to strike.

Who had been waiting—waiting for the proper moment. She jumped to her feet and hissed in sudden fury, "Get out!" He was a stranger; he didn't know her. What right did he have to question her?

Amusement played about the man's sensual mouth as he leisurely uncoiled his long length from the chair. "I'm not condemning, mind you. Making love in the out-of-doors can be very . . . stimulating. I'm just asking if you ever do it conventionally—in a bed."

JoAnna stamped her foot in outraged dignity. "I said get out!"

"I'm going." The maddening smile disappeared at last and he started to move away. But as he did, something made JoAnna demand: "Why did you stop him? If you thought that about us, why did you do it?"

The man halted halfway to the door and the gaze he directed toward her was level. "Let's just say it was because I wasn't sure."

"Well, thank you for that at least!" JoAnna snapped shortly.

The man dipped his dark head in acknowledgment.

JoAnna waited for him to leave. She was tired of men—all men—and when he continued to stand there and look at her, she raised her chin a degree and reminded him coolly, "I've asked you to leave."

"I will . . . in a minute. But first there's something I want you to know. If you mean to go on the way you have been, keep away from the front of my house. I'm not a prude—far from it—but I don't appreciate looking out my window and seeing you lying on the sand with one of your boyfriends in various stages of the sex act!"

More shocked than she had ever been before in her life, JoAnna retorted through clenched teeth, "The beaches in

Texas are free. They're public domain. You can't stop me from doing what I like, where I like." She didn't care what he thought of her now. He was the most hateful man she had ever met!

"I can for the purposes you're using them" came the unfeeling reply. "Ever hear of public indecency?"

JoAnna almost exploded. Never—ever—had any man talked to her in this way. And never—ever—had she experienced a day like today. First Alice Cole, then Philip, and now this man who claimed to be her neighbor! And it wasn't even noon yet!

With fury in every step, JoAnna stalked around him to open the door pointedly. Once there she glared at him wordlessly.

The man smiled slightly, a half smile that was filled with derision as his eyes made a leisurely tour of her rigidly held body. "For new neighbors, I'd say we've gotten off to a pretty bad start," he commented dryly.

Holding his eyes defiantly, JoAnna refused to make a reply.

"And since we're the *only* neighbors for miles around, we have to be either good friends or bad enemies."

JoAnna lifted her chin, her emerald eyes flashing a heated message, letting him know in no uncertain terms her answer to his implied question.

The man shrugged and moved on, remarking as if to himself, "Oh, well, can't win 'em all, I guess."

As soon as his back was barely clear of the door, JoAnna slammed it shut with all the force she could muster, hoping that he would suffer the aftershock of her displeasure. Somehow, in some way, she felt as if she had to strike back at a day that had been so hurtful and at the man who had been the last emissary of that hurt.

CHAPTER TWO

The rest of the weekend proved uneventful, which was a relief to JoAnna after Saturday morning. No one called, no visitors came to see her—either friendly or unfriendly—and she was left to deal with her hurt alone. Of her new neighbor she saw nothing. She was careful to stay away from her windows even when she heard his car start up and drive away, which happened frequently Saturday afternoon and all day Sunday.

The result of his numerous trips greeted her Monday morning when she descended her stairs for work. Lumber of assorted sizes and lengths, aluminum window frames, rolls of tar paper, stacks of shingles, all were grouped and waiting on the sand beside his house. What was the man planning to do? she asked herself as she unlocked her garage door. Rebuild his entire beach house? If so, that would mean he was going to be around for some time—something she had heartily hoped he would not.

JoAnna was frowning as she slid into the driver's seat of her car and laid her purse and the scarlet jacket that matched her skirt on the seat beside her. She turned the key in the ignition and waited for the motor's usual hum. But this time the engine refused to behave as she expected and the grinding noise continued.

After a full ten minutes of trying, JoAnna had to finally admit defeat, especially when, as a result of her last try, the engine would not turn over at all. Helplessly, she began to beat her fists against the steering wheel. What was she going to do? She had to get to work. Slowly her eyes were drawn to the beach house a short distance away. He was there; she knew he was. His car was parked in the drive.

"Good friends or bad enemies." His words echoed in her mind and she chewed at her bottom lip. She had given him her answer to that statement and she had meant it—she still did. But what did this situation fall under? Did enemies help one another when one was in difficulty?

JoAnna straightened her shoulders and slid from the seat to begin the difficult walk toward his house. It was going to be hard to swallow her pride and ask for a favor, but she had to do it. She only wondered what his reaction was going to be. Would he slam his door in her face as soon as he saw who was calling?

JoAnna skirted the building materials gingerly and mounted the stairs that led to his door. Several stairs creaked ominously under her slight weight, and she wondered how in the world a man of his size ever climbed them. Paint was almost nonexistent on the weathered exterior, and what there was of it was peeling in a not very attractive manner.

When she bought her beach house, the owner told her the house next door had been built long ago by a man who was very old and seldom came. In the four years that she had lived there, the man's words had proved true. No one came—not even to check on the place. And as a result the storms and squalls had taken their toll.

Several panes of glass were broken in the narrow windows that flanked the door and the only thing that had saved the large sliding glass door that faced the beach from breakage was a dilapidated piece of plywood someone must have nailed up before a hurricane and forgotten to take down. Now it was hanging drunkenly by one nail and lodged sideways, partially blocking half of the verandah. There were no window curtains, and from within JoAnna could smell the tantalizing aroma of coffee and freshly fried bacon. Just as she raised a hand to knock, the sound of masculine whistling floated through the air, momentarily causing her to pause.

JoAnna took a deep breath and swallowed hard, twice, then knocked.

Heavy footsteps jarred the flooring, making her think that her new neighbor was right in one thing at least—he did badly need to repair the house. She only hoped the pilings it was balanced on could withstand her added presence for the few moments she planned to stay.

She wiped all traces of expression from her features as the door was swept open and the man's large form filled the doorway.

"Ahhh . . . I thought it might be you. What's the matter? Having car trouble?"

JoAnna raised her chin and asked sweetly, "Are you clairvoyant too?"

"No, just able to hear. Battery gone dead?"

JoAnna gave a short nod.

The man stepped back and motioned for her to come in. JoAnna shook her head hastily. "No—thank you. I only wanted to see . . . if you have a jumper cable and would mind helping me." She finished the sentence in a rush, then glared at the flicker of amusement she saw pull at the man's hard mouth. Today he was dressed in what must be his usual uniform: cut-off jeans and nothing else. She wondered if he even knew what a shirt was!

"Sure, I'll help you. But you're going to have to wait a few minutes. I just made breakfast. Come on in." At her hesitation he prompted, "We could call a temporary truce, if you like."

Feeling slightly ridiculous, JoAnna agreed, but it was with some sense of wariness that she stepped into the room. As far as furniture went, it contained the bare minimum—a chair, a small wooden table, a battery-operated lantern that was sitting unused on the floor. . . . JoAnna moved stiffly across the room.

"Would you like something to eat? Coffee?"

She shook her head no to each.

The man shrugged and moved into another room that must be his kitchen. Unlike her house, there was no open breakfast bar separating the two rooms. He came out again almost immediately with a plate containing eggs and several slices of crisp bacon. He sat the plate down on the small table, then straddled the chair.

"I'm a little short on nonessentials—like furniture, electricity, a telephone. . . . Do you have a phone?"

JoAnna moved restlessly as she watched him begin to tuck into his food. She hadn't felt much like eating anything all weekend, merely picking at the frozen dinners she had heated. Now, watching him stow it away with such obvious enjoyment, her stomach started to protest. She subdued it forcefully.

"Yes, I have one." Her answer was cool. She felt a small niggle of conscience at not offering its services to him as he seemed to be hinting, especially when she was asking a favor, but her memory of what he had said to her Saturday made it an easy matter to ignore.

"Are you going to work?"

"Yes."

He shot her a narrowed look. "Where do you work, in Galveston?"

"Yes."

"Are you with the Secret Service?"

This question startled JoAnna out of her determined calm.

"What?"

"The Secret Service. You're obviously a pro at giving away very little information."

JoAnna's eyes widened and she answered stiffly, "I didn't know you expected me to tell you my life's story. After all, I don't really know you."

The man's strong white teeth crunched into a piece of bacon. After dispensing with it with a great deal of satisfaction, he murmured tauntingly, "And since we are in a state of war—"

"Exactly . . . by your choice."

"Oh, no, not mine. Normally I'm the easiest person in the world to get along with."

JoAnna stared at him mutely. She knew that had to be a lie. You could tell just by looking at him that he expected things to go his way and that they usually did. It was a part of him, just like breathing.

She gave a small sigh, her patience wearing thin. "Look, Mr. . . ." Suddenly she realized that she didn't know his name. She looked at him blankly.

"Morgan, Luke Morgan."

JoAnna acknowledged his words with one part of her brain but went on with what she had started. "I don't want to rush you, but I'm already late. If you take much longer, I might as well not go in."

"I'm almost finished. Relax."

"I can't relax! My employer expects me to be at work by eight o'clock and it's almost nine now."

"Have you called in?"

"Of course."

"Well, then I don't see what your problem is."

JoAnna's patience snapped. "I don't care *what* you see or don't see, Mr. Morgan. All I ask is that you hurry!"

"Eating too fast is bad for your digestion."

"And so is. . . . Oh, I give up! I'll go call a taxi. I should have known better than to ask you for help!"

He was on his feet before she had taken two steps. "Calm down—I'm done. If you're in that much of a hurry, I can run you in myself."

JoAnna was breathing hard. She told herself it was because she was angry, but in truth it was more than that. She had met this man only two days before but he could get under her skin faster than any person she had ever known.

Valiantly she fought for control. "No . . . that won't be necessary."

"You were the one worried about being late," he reminded her.

JoAnna chanced a quick glance at her watch. The minute hand seemed to be flying.

"Oh, God," she groaned.

"If you give me your keys, I'll see what I can do about your car while you're at work. It may not be just the battery."

Knowing that to be true since the car had been giving her trouble for the last week or two, JoAnna closed her eyes. It meant further concessions to the enemy, but right now getting to her job was more important.

"All right, thank you," she finally agreed.

Luke Morgan's hard face relaxed into an engaging grin. "See, that wasn't so bad, was it?"

Instantly JoAnna regretted the decision, but she held her tongue out of necessity.

The trip from the west end of Galveston Island into the city proper took the better part of a half hour. Most of it had been accomplished in silence on JoAnna's part and a tuneful humming on Luke Morgan's. He had apologized that he had no car radio and then proceeded to try to make up for it by giving his renditions of all the popular songs of the day. JoAnna could have screamed.

Tourists were out in numbers as they drove along Seawall Boulevard—bicycling, roller skating, running, some even walking on the elevated sidewalk that ran along the water's edge. The wall had been built to provide protection for the most populated section of the island after the terrible storm of 1900 that had devastated the city, but now it provided an excellent gathering place for visitors and natives alike. Surfers were out trying to find the elusive "big wave" that never occurred in the relative calm of the Galveston surf. The only time the waves were any way near ideal was when a hurricane was offshore whipping up the winds and water. And then surfing was discouraged by worried officials.

JoAnna gave directions to a now-silent Luke Morgan, who was having to give more of his attention to dealing with traffic and less to humming.

When the car stopped in front of the familiar two-story brick building where she worked, JoAnna gathered her purse and jacket and smoothed down her wind-blown hair. Air-conditioning was something else his Ford Bronco did not have. The windows had been open and she felt as if she had been sitting inside a wind tunnel facing the wrong direction.

"What time do you get off work?" Luke asked as she hurried to open the door.

"What?"

With exaggerated patience he repeated his question.

"Oh! You don't have to come get me. I can get a ride home with one of my friends . . . one of my girl friends," she hastened to add when she saw his eyebrow rise. Now why had she done that? she asked herself disgustedly. What he thought didn't matter a fig to her!

"I'm going to be coming into town again later anyway, so why make someone waste a trip?"

JoAnna could have stayed arguing with him all day but she didn't have the time. It was close to nine thirty, and as it was she would probably have to work through lunch.

"Oh, all right! Come pick me up!" She knew it was ungracious but that was the way he affected her.

"I thought you'd see it my way" was his maddening reply.

The light of battle entered JoAnna's emerald eyes. "Be here at four," she called, tumbling from the car.

"Okay, see you then."

JoAnna closed the door with a restrained motion, then forced herself to hold on to her hard-won control until she was safely through the tall glass doors of her building. But once inside she released her pent-up tension by leaning against the wall and giving way to a wholly wicked snicker of laughter.

"And just see how you like waiting for half an hour, Mr. Know-it-all Luke Morgan!" she challenged, her eyes flashing and her honey-blond curls tossing in defiance. Then she ran the short distance to the stairs and mounted them as fast as her three-inch heels would allow.

Melissa Connelly was busy typing when JoAnna walked in through the office door.

"Better late than never, I always say," the girl teased, pausing in her work.

JoAnna tucked her purse away in her bottom desk drawer and struggled into her jacket.

"Was Mr. Daniels very upset?"

"Not any more than he usually is when you're not here. Get your car fixed?"

JoAnna took the cover off her typewriter and glanced at the stack of folders and correspondence that awaited her.

"Not exactly."

Melissa's blue eyes gazed at her questioningly. "How did you get here then? Surely you didn't try to walk—not from the back of beyond where you live."

Hastily JoAnna ran a comb through her hair, patting it into place from memory rather than searching for the hand mirror that was somewhere in her middle drawer.

"I have a new neighbor. He brought me in." Her tone clearly warned that she didn't want further questions, but as a friend of long standing, Melissa ignored it.

"He?"

"He." JoAnna picked up the phone memo pad. "Mr. Summers called?"

Melissa finally took the hint, but the glint of determination in her eyes promised that eventually she would resume her line of questioning.

"At eight sharp. Mr. Daniels told him *you* had all the info."

"Mr. Daniels is a frightened sheep."

"My, we are out of sorts, aren't we?"

"Shut up, Lissa."

Melissa grinned and turned away, beginning to hum a pop tune to herself.

"And don't do that, please!"

"Sorry!" The set of her friend's shoulders told JoAnna that she had been too sharp. She sighed deeply and apologized.

"The last few days have been hell, Lissa. My nerves are a little shot."

Melissa frowned, her round, freckled face serious as she sensed JoAnna had problems other than her car.

"Would you like to talk later?" she prompted.

"Maybe. I don't know," JoAnna replied abstractedly, reaching for the top folder and opening it.

Her friend's rust-colored head nodded thoughtfully, then the telephone rang and prevented further conversation.

Just as she thought, JoAnna had to work through lunch. Melissa offered to stay and help but JoAnna firmly refused. Melissa was meeting her fiancé, who was in town on leave from an oil-drilling platform located far out in the Gulf where he worked as part of the production team, and she didn't want to interfere. The two of them had so little time together what with Bill's schedule being what it was —two weeks on the rig and two weeks off—and then he had to spend part of his leave time with his elderly parents. Each moment they were able to spend together was like gold to them. And anyway, JoAnna knew working would help her not to think.

Ever since Saturday her thoughts had been chaotic. But

what aggravated her the most was that Philip played so little a part in them. The main star seemed to be her new neighbor. And that was stupid! She didn't know him and what little she had discovered, she didn't like! With fierce determination she plunged into the remaining work.

By late afternoon she was almost caught up with her work, and since Mr. Daniels had finally scuffled away to meet with a client, the office was at last peaceful.

Melissa and JoAnna shared the office but did not share Mr. Daniels. JoAnna was his secretary and technically Melissa was her assistant. But even though Melissa was an excellent secretary in her own right, Mr. Daniels almost had apoplexy whenever JoAnna had time off—an occurrence that was scheduled in two weeks' time. So already he was starting to become a little shaky. Sometimes JoAnna and Melissa would share a giggle and a wry comment about their employer, but in truth both of them liked him. Maternal instinct, JoAnna thought humorously. But for all his bumbling ways and timidity, Mr. Daniels was an extremely able accountant, keeping the books of a number of small businesses in the area.

When JoAnna pulled the last sheet of paper from her IBM, she stretched and yawned hugely.

Melissa looked up from her filing and grinned. "I didn't think you were ever going to surface."

JoAnna smiled back tiredly. "Neither did I. What time is it anyway?" She glanced at her wrist, answering her own question. "Four thirty." She stared at her watch disbelievingly.

Melissa nodded. "Aren't you hungry? I started to run down to the deli and smuggle a sandwich back but I was afraid you'd refuse to touch it until you were done. Would you like one now?"

JoAnna rubbed a weary hand over the back of her aching neck. "No—thanks, though. I'm not particularly hungry."

Melissa closed the file drawer and came to perch on the edge of JoAnna's desk.

"Want to talk about what's been bothering you?" she asked quietly, her blue eyes soft with concern.

"Not really...." JoAnna sighed, then at Melissa's hurt look she relented and murmured dryly, "I guess I just don't want you to be able to say 'I told you so.'"

Melissa was alert instantly. "It's Philip," she stated rather than asked.

"Who else?" JoAnna quipped, the image of a form much more muscular than Philip's immediately coming into her mind. She pushed it aside with an imperceptible shake of her head.

"What happened? Did you finally see what a rat he is?"

JoAnna's green eyes retained a shadow of hurt. "I guess you could say that. He's married, Lissa."

"You mean he wasn't divorced like he told you?"

"No—and . . . his wife is going to have their baby."

Melissa didn't have red hair for nothing. She sucked in a deep breath and positively bristled. "I knew I could smell something each time he walked in through the door! How could he do something like that to you? That dirty—"

"It's over, Lissa," JoAnna interrupted, putting a calming hand on her friend's arm. "I'm not going to see him again."

Melissa's mouth snapped shut. "How did you find out? I doubt that *he* told you."

JoAnna looked away. "His wife came to see me."

"Oh, God! That must have been awful for you."

"Well, it wasn't very pretty," JoAnna admitted wryly.

"Was she upset? Did she try to scratch your eyes out?" Melissa had a very vivid imagination, and as that was what she would have done to any woman foolish enough to try to take Bill away from her . . .

"No, it was all very civilized."

Melissa shook her head. "No wonder you were in a foul mood this morning. When did you see her?"

"Saturday."

"You poor kid! You could have called. I would have come out to be with you. You shouldn't have spent the rest of the weekend alone."

JoAnna shrugged.

Melissa was silent for a moment, then she picked up a pencil and began to tap the eraser on her nylon-clad knee. "There's an old saying that applies here . . ." she began, but she stopped as JoAnna pursed her lips and tilted her head.

"Isn't there always? And you know them all, don't you?"

Melissa answered with pretended haughty superiority, "Yes." She pointed the pencil directly at JoAnna's face. "And this one applies to you."

"Come on, get it over with!"

"A hair of the dog!" she pronounced proudly.

JoAnna looked confused. "What?"

"A hair of the dog! A hair of the dog that bit you!"

"Melissa, I think you've been standing in the sun too long. What *are* you talking about?"

Melissa slid from the desk and straightened her skirt.

Her eyes were speculative as she studied JoAnna's face. "Bill has a friend—"

"Oh, no! Oh, no!" JoAnna began to shake her head. "Now I know what you're doing. And the answer is no! I'm off men—for good!"

Melissa smiled. "That won't last long." She walked around behind JoAnna's chair.

"No, I mean it, I've had it with men!" JoAnna swiveled her chair to follow her friend's movements. Melissa had paused at the window. Something on the street below must have caught her attention because she became absolutely still, her entire concentration centering on what was happening there.

JoAnna watched her curiously for a moment before joining her. "What's—" She got no further with her question because instantly she had her answer.

Philip was there, his perfectly combed hair for once mussed as his head was lolling backward, the neck of his shirt and tie caught in an iron grip by the clenched fingers of Luke Morgan. The man was practically lifting Philip in the air, and that was no easy feat because Philip was almost as tall as he.

"Oh," JoAnna breathed softly. Frozen, Melissa couldn't turn away from the tableau below.

While they watched, Luke Morgan's lips began to move, then he gave Philip a shake and tossed him away as if he were nothing more than a rag doll. Philip staggered back and hit the concrete hard on the seat of his pants, his arms flying out as he tried to gain some semblance of balance.

Under the girls' fascinated gaze, Luke Morgan turned away and walked the short distance back to his car, leaning against the fender and crossing his arms securely over his chest. Philip scuttled to his feet, his hands rolled into fists, his battered body stiff.

Luke Morgan glanced at him as if he were an angry fly.

Philip hovered for a moment in indecision, then he settled for a hurled word instead of more physical contact. Luke Morgan ignored him. Philip waited for another moment, then turned and stalked away, his taut movements those of blustery defeat.

JoAnna's eyes followed Philip as he walked away but obviously Melissa's had not.

"My Lord," she breathed, her blue gaze fixed on the dark-haired man below, taking in the lean, powerful body that was encased in form-fitting tan cords and a wide-striped white, tan, and blue pullover shirt. "Who in the world is that—in the words of my thirteen-year-old niece —hunk?"

Hesitantly JoAnna allowed her gaze to shift back to the waiting man. In her absorption of trying to finish her day's work, she had totally forgotten about telling him to come early. And now, seeing him, her conscience pricked her.

He looked so calm standing there. Not as if he had just been a participant in a fight—although to call what had happened a fight was glorifying it. It had been too one-sided for a fight.

A nameless shiver ran down JoAnna's spine. She cleared her throat nervously, acknowledging to herself that witnessing what had transpired had upset her more than she realized. "He—he's my new neighbor."

Melissa turned to stare at her blankly.

"He moved in to the house next to mine," JoAnna explained unnecessarily. Melissa was staring at her so strangely that JoAnna tried to smile dismissingly. Yet her heart was beating at a faster rate and she felt a pinkening of her cheeks.

"Your neighbor," Melissa repeated flatly.

JoAnna nodded, moving away from the window after another glance at Luke Morgan.

"The man who brought you to work this morning."

JoAnna nodded again, clearing the pencils and bits of loose paper from the top of her desk and putting them into her middle drawer. For some reason she couldn't meet Melissa's eyes.

"Why was he fighting with Philip?"

The telephone rang and JoAnna grasped it desperately. But when the conversation was over, Melissa was still waiting, the set of her chin informing JoAnna that she was prepared to wait all night.

JoAnna sighed. "He, well . . . Philip. . . ." She sank slowly into her chair. "Philip didn't take it too well when I told him we were through." A master of understatement, she thought, then giggled almost insanely as she remembered Luke Morgan's earlier sardonic question, asking her if she worked for the Secret Service. Maybe they could use her. She was certainly learning to evade delicate questions.

Melissa noted the flicker of JoAnna's lips and filed it away in her mind. "So how does that involve your neighbor?"

"H-he had to help me persuade Philip to leave."

"Hmmm. I have the feeling I'm not getting the entire story, but maybe it's for the best. Philip looks as if he has enough on his hands without adding your brothers and Bill as well."

JoAnna remained conspicuously silent.

The ride home began much as the ride in the morning,

except the rear of the Bronco was filled with more building materials and Luke Morgan was quiet.

Ever since taking her seat next to him, JoAnna had waited uncomfortably for him to mention either his enforced half-hour wait or his meeting with Philip—but it seemed he would do neither. He had greeted her with a short nod and then promptly busied himself with pulling into the stream of afternoon traffic as if this had been the hundredth time he had picked her up from work rather than the first.

As they drove back along Seawall Boulevard, retracing their morning's journey, some of the tension finally began to leave JoAnna's body and she closed her eyes, savoring the breeze that blew through her blond curls rather than cursing it as she had earlier. It had been a long, tiring day on the heels of a difficult weekend and anything that refreshed her mind and spirit was welcome.

"You haven't asked me about your car."

The words caught JoAnna unaware and she sat up straighter, her eyes flying open in confusion.

"My car?"

Luke Morgan nodded, mercifully keeping any sarcastic comments to himself. "The coil wire had come loose."

JoAnna pretended to brush a piece of lint from her skirt, trying to cover her embarrassment at being caught out. She certainly didn't want to admit to him that she knew nothing about the insides of a car. All she knew was that periodically a car required feeding and checks on the air pressure of the tires. The rest she left to the garage on the infrequent occasions she had need of one.

"Is that very serious?" She tried to sound cool and collected.

Her effort was not very successful. Glancing away from

the oncoming traffic, Luke Morgan shot her a look of masculine amusement. "No," he drawled easily, "except the motor won't run very well without it—not at all, in fact. But fixing it is just a simple matter of reconnecting the wire." JoAnna concentrated on the stubborn piece of nonexistent lint. "But you do need a tuneup," he continued. "The engine needs a lot of adjustment."

JoAnna nodded and gave a feeble "I guess I'll have to see about it then" before turning to look out the passenger window.

They proceeded on for several more blocks before he spoke again. "You hungry?"

JoAnna's stomach answered for itself, choosing that particular moment to give an embarrassing growl. She couldn't blame it really. It had received only a small piece of toast at breakfast and nothing since.

Luke Morgan laughed outright, his white teeth flashing. "I guess that means yes."

An answering smile began to pull at JoAnna's finely molded lips. Then she couldn't help it; she laughed with him.

His twinkling eyes rested on her appreciatively, taking in the soft curve of her cheek and small, straight nose. He pulled the car over into a slow lane and began to look for a restaurant.

"Living on an island, I suppose you like fish."

"Love it."

"I thought so. It so happens that I do too. What do you think about eating here?"

He had slowed in front of a well-known restaurant that specialized in seafood.

"Fine. But there's one thing. I want to pay for my own meal."

"Spoken like a true liberated lady," he teased.

It was only when they were seated at a table and waiting for their order to be taken that JoAnna realized he had not agreed to her request. She started to bring the matter up again but he forestalled her by asking her opinion of one of the dishes on the menu.

Their meal was delicious—a smorgasbord of seafoods fresh from the Gulf and prepared to the finest turn: crab, shrimp, flounder, red fish. . . . JoAnna found herself enjoying her meal. She was hungry for the first time in days and made healthy inroads on the food before her.

After some time Luke Morgan sat back with a contented sigh and smiled as JoAnna forked a slippery oyster from its shell.

"I like to see a woman enjoy her food," he pronounced, which had the immediate effect of making JoAnna feel like a pig.

She put the oyster in her mouth anyway and smiled sweetly as she swallowed it.

"So do I—especially when it's me."

He acknowledged her parry. "I met your friend today."

JoAnna became still. "Oh?" she answered carefully, not about to tell him that she had seen it all from her office window.

"He was on his way to see you."

JoAnna blinked, her emerald eyes cloudy.

"I stopped him—working on the idea that you really meant it when you said you didn't want to see him again."

JoAnna raised her chin, the pleasantness of the last half hour beginning to dissipate. "I did mean it."

He regarded her steadily. "I don't think you'll have to worry about him bothering you again then."

JoAnna frowned, something about the answer being too pat, too easy, raising her suspicions.

"Why?" she asked cautiously.

"Because I told him you were my girl friend now."

"What?" JoAnna squeaked.

"You heard me. Oh, you know it's not true and I know it's not true—but he doesn't."

For the second time in as many days, JoAnna was almost beyond speech. "Why you . . . you . . ." she sputtered. Finally, getting her unruly tongue organized, she cried, "You had no right to do that! No right!"

"Then you didn't mean what you said?" His pale eyes glittered into her own, his mouth a thin line.

JoAnna bit her bottom lip. How could you win with this man? For a moment she had forgotten how hateful he could be. Forgotten what he thought about her and her morals—or lack of them.

"I want to go home now," she answered stiffly, opening her purse and withdrawing several bills. "Here, here's my part of the check."

The man looked at her steadily, as if gauging her seriousness, then with a slight shrug he reached out one large hand and took the money.

"I was going to suggest that you repay me by inviting me to a home-cooked meal. I'm bound to get a little tired of what I'm able to fix on my camp stove. I don't have any idea of when I'll finally be able to get the electricity turned on." He paused. "But I suppose that's out now."

JoAnna positively glared at him. "You suppose right."

Luke firmed his jaw and motioned for the waiter. Once the bill was paid, he ushered her out through the tables, scrupulously keeping a good two-foot distance between them.

JoAnna moved jerkily, her temper seething, not alert to the man who was entering the restaurant and talking animatedly with a friend. Suddenly he careened into her, causing her to bounce back against Luke's hard body. Instantly Luke's hands came up and drew her close in order to steady her—and for several heart-pounding seconds blood thundered in JoAnna's ears, rioting out of control, her breath seeming to catch somewhere in her throat. Then he was setting her free, and it was everything she could do just to act as if nothing out of the ordinary had happened. Her heart was beating ridiculously fast and her senses were swimming. Convulsively she tightened her grip on her purse.

"Oh, I'm dreadfully sorry. Did I hurt you?" the man who bumped into her apologized, his voice thick with a strong British accent.

JoAnna stared up into the long, narrow face totally at a loss, unable to answer because her emotions were churning so.

"I expect she'll survive" came Luke's dry comment from close behind. Then he gave a firm push on her back that sent her out the glass-and-chrome door and into the large parking area.

She would survive, Luke had said; but after that cataclysmic experience of only a moment before, JoAnna was less sure.

CHAPTER THREE

That night JoAnna paced across her living-room floor feeling something like a caged lioness. *What was the matter with her?* she asked herself for the hundredth time in the space of an hour. Was she some kind of nymphomaniac who was attracted to any available male?

Just three days ago she had thought herself wildly in love with Philip . . . and now? No, she shook her head emphatically, she couldn't call it love. Love didn't enter into the tidal wave of feeling she had experienced when held close to Luke Morgan's hard, powerful body.

And she didn't even like the man!

It was silly, it was crazy—yet it was something she could not ignore. Even thinking about it now recalled vividly the heady sensations that had flooded her unsuspecting form.

Sexual desire, she admitted with brutal honesty. She wasn't exactly a stranger to it. She had experienced it before, with Philip. But she had excused herself with the notion that she loved him. And that had made it okay to her uptight little puritan soul.

But Luke Morgan!! What was she? An animal? A bitch in heat? *No!* Her chin came up in determination. She would control herself, control her feelings. It shouldn't be all that hard, she consoled herself bracingly. She would stay away from the man, and as Lissa would say: out of sight, out of mind. She knew his opinion of her and knew that that was where the danger lay. If he should ever find out that she was attracted to him. . . .

JoAnna shuddered uncontrollably, a thrill of fear as well as excitement darkening her emerald-green eyes. In her mind's eye a vision of Luke Morgan refused to be dismissed, just as it had since she first met him. His ruggedly handsome face, those pale eyes that one moment could look quizzical, the next teasing, and the next cold and icy. The long hard length of him that his more conventional clothing of today had emphasized rather than hidden. His muscular thighs that had strained against the material of his corded jeans, the taut hips and flat stomach, those wide, powerful shoulders and well-developed upper arms. And his muscles were not just for show. He was strong. He had lifted Philip as if he were nothing more than a toy!

In spite of herself, JoAnna's mind skipped on to wondering what it would be like to be crushed in those arms. To feel his mouth take savage possession of her own, to have his hands run demandingly, urgently over her body. . . .

Suddenly disgusted with herself, JoAnna groaned. God! She had to stop thinking about the man!

For the remainder of the week, JoAnna was pretty successful. She left her house extremely early each morning, arriving at work a full hour ahead of time, and in the evenings she shopped and took turns visiting her older brothers and their families—one of whom she had to make the hour-long drive in to Houston to see. But to achieve her goal, she was willing to do anything. Her only problem seemed to be that she was wearing herself out. Burning the candle at both ends soon began to tell on her. She explained to her brothers that she had broken up with Philip and they had been both sympathetic and relieved. She had introduced Philip once at a family get-together and had immediately felt the constrained tension that resulted from her brothers' instant dislike.

Deceiving Melissa was another problem all together. They had been friends for the past four years and Melissa was too well endowed with feminine intuition, as well as knowledge of JoAnna, to be fooled for long.

"Hair of the dog work yet?" she asked airily one morning while JoAnna was concentrating on changing the ribbon of her typewriter.

JoAnna looked up startled, her face immediately turning pink.

Melissa made a considering moue of her generous mouth. "I told you it would," she bragged smugly.

"I hate to disappoint you, but you're wrong this time, Lissa," JoAnna replied after hastily gathering her scattered wits. "I'm not having anything to do with either men or dogs."

"We'll see."

"I'm not!"

Melissa only smiled benignly and buried her nose back in her file drawer.

Saturday morning JoAnna planned to sleep late. She had been so tired the previous evening she had barely been able to complete her bath. But as on all the previous nights of that week, once she was in bed and there was nothing else to demand her attention, she thought of the man next door.

Some mornings her bed sheets looked as if a battle had taken place the night before—and one had. Restless, JoAnna would turn from stomach to back to side, in a vain effort to conjure up sheep rather than Luke Morgan. She usually became successful sometime during the early hours of the morning.

Friday night had proved no different from the rest. Her last disgusted glance at her bedside clock showed that it was some time after four before she finally managed to evict his haunting image. So it was that she was in a state of absolute exhaustion when the loud hammering coming from across the way shattered her hard-won rest with vivid brutality.

At first JoAnna covered her head with her pillow, trying to blot out the annoying sound. Then, finding that unsuccessful, she groped for her clock and squinted her eyes, trying to make the white numerals become clear. It said it was the ungodly hour of 7 A.M. Three hours! Three lousy hours!

With the sweet disposition of a grizzly bear disturbed from her winter's nap, JoAnna rolled out of her bed. It would be impossible to try to sleep further with all that noise going on!

She staggered into her kitchen and put the kettle on for a cup of much-needed coffee. Her head was pounding, echoing each successive strike of the hammer.

Finally the hammering stopped, but the silence only lasted for a few seconds. Then it started up again. Repeatedly for the next half hour, the hammering began, then ended, then began again. JoAnna thought she was going to go crazy!

Even though she didn't want them, she tried to eat a bowl of corn flakes, hoping that the crunchy cereal would give the woodpecker next door some competition. But all too soon the milk turned the flakes into mush, and she pushed the bowl away in annoyance.

She tried the radio but her sensitive ears seemed to be attuned to each successive blow of the hammer.

Finally, in desperation, JoAnna marched into her bedroom and changed into a pair of lemon-yellow shorts and a matching terry tank top. There was only one thing to do. She had to get away!

Up until this last weekend JoAnna had spent much of her free time away from work wandering along the beach, hunting for unusual shells and bits and pieces of driftwood that sometimes wash ashore. She enjoyed making pictures and unusual sculptures with what she found and sometimes sold her work on consignment at a local gift shop. But mostly she did it for enjoyment.

When she stepped out onto her verandah this morning, the wind blew briskly against her slender body and ruffled her short golden curls, making her realize just what she had been sacrificing over the last week in trying to avoid her neighbor. She loved the beach. She had lived here ever since her parents had died, leaving her to rattle around alone in a large house that seemed all the more vacant because of the memories it held.

As the youngest of four children, JoAnna could scarcely remember a time when there had not been laughter and noise in the house. Then one by one her older brothers went off to college or married and soon she was the only babe left in the nest. But still the house had been filled with either her friends or her parents' multitude of friends and she had never felt lonely. Then one beautiful, soft spring day when she was twenty, her oldest brother, Bob, came to tell her that their parents had been killed in a freeway accident while on their way to vacation with friends in New Mexico.

JoAnna's world was never the same; change followed change.

Already close to her brothers, she became more so. It was as if they instinctively felt they had to band together—the only remaining Davis issue.

The house had been sold and JoAnna found this beach house. Her brothers had not liked the idea of her living in so isolated an area—they had tried to persuade her to move in with one of them. But JoAnna resisted. Strangely enough, the isolation was what she needed. She could never have stayed alone in the family home; but here, in a different house with no memories, she could be happy. And she was.

A loud whistling had now joined the sound of the hammering. Turning in the direction of the neighboring beach house, JoAnna narrowed her eyes against the bright morning glare.

Luke Morgan was sitting on his roof, stripped to the waist, wearing his usual cut-offs, happily and loudly adding another sand-colored shingle to the row he had already attached.

Obviously he's never heard of peace and quiet, JoAnna thought sourly to herself. She stuffed her hands in the pockets of her shorts and began a slow descent down her exterior stairs. Once on the sand, she turned sharply to walk toward the water, keeping her eyes firmly on the ground, hoping that she would not be noticed.

"Hey! You!" The commanding voice halted her.

She looked up, gritting her teeth. "Did you say something?" she asked sweetly.

Luke Morgan flashed a roguish smile and walked over to the edge of the roof. With pantherish ease and absolutely no fear, he lowered himself until he was sitting down, his legs swinging over the side.

JoAnna swallowed tightly, never having been very brave where heights were concerned.

"I haven't seen you all week," he commented.

"That's funny. I haven't seen you either," JoAnna retorted smartly. She tried to avoid looking at him, instead letting her eyes run assessingly over the work he had accomplished over the last few days.

The beach house was certainly beginning to look like something now. The stairs had been rebuilt and sported a new coat of white paint. The broken windows had been replaced with new ones that gave the verandah a jaunty air. The old piece of plywood had been removed and now the sliding door was opened invitingly to the Gulf breeze. JoAnna raised a delicate eyebrow. He certainly hadn't waited until today to start work, that was more than evident.

"I didn't wake you up, did I?" The question from above caused her to look up, her expression incredulous. On seeing her unbelieving look, Luke hurried on, "Listen, if I did, I'm sorry. I didn't think about it being Saturday until I saw you. I wanted to get an early start on this, so. . . ." He shrugged his powerful sun-bronzed shoulders.

JoAnna swallowed. She tried to tell herself that it was seeing him sitting so nonchalantly two stories above the ground that made her breath come more quickly, but she knew that wasn't entirely the truth.

"Just so long as you're not planning to do it again

tomorrow morning," she mumbled, her attention shifting to a gull that swooped close by.

"I should be done with this by then. Anyway, I don't work on Sundays." He paused, then startled her by saying, "Did you know you have an advantage over me?" When JoAnna switched her puzzled gaze back to him, he gave her a smile of such charm that she felt her heart leap. "You know my name, but I don't know yours. And unless you want me to keep calling you 'hey you' . . ." He let the sentence finish itself.

"My name is JoAnna Davis," JoAnna answered primly, feeling distinctly priggish.

"Nice name."

"I'm glad you approve. Didn't you say you wanted to finish this job today?"

His pale eyes narrowed. "Is that a hint?"

"I suppose you could say it is."

"What am I keeping you from? An assignation somewhere farther down the beach?"

JoAnna failed in her attempt to count to ten. "Yes! Of course!" she snapped. "And I don't want to make him wait!"

Luke got to his feet with athletic grace. "Well, don't let me stop you then." He turned away, intent on taking up where he had left off in his work.

JoAnna spun around on her heels, her temper sputtering. How in the world could she be attracted to someone as hateful as that? She had covered half the distance to the water, dark thoughts about him falling off his damned roof filling her mind, when his voice called to her again. "Hey! JoAnna!"

Her shoulders stiffened.

"Could I use your telephone?" he called. "Mine won't

be installed for a while yet and I have an important call to make."

JoAnna felt like telling him to get in his car and drive to town if he needed to make a call, but instead she nodded her head in curt assent. Her mother had drilled manners in to her with too much enthusiasm.

JoAnna spent the better part of the next two hours walking along the beach, and gradually, as she walked, her headache began to disappear, the fresh air working its usual miracle. Periodically she passed weekenders, people who came from Houston and its surrounding suburbs to spend the day, and an occasional tourist intent on getting a tan at the expense of severely sunburned skin. Children played in the shallow water and at the water's edge building castles and searching for shells.

Once she passed near a man of about her age who was setting up a catamaran. He glanced across at her, his eyes running appreciatively over her slender yet softly rounded figure. He asked if she would like to take a sail. JoAnna smiled, shook her head, and kept walking.

Much later, when she returned to the spot where the man had launched his boat, she could see the variegated stripes of his orange-and-white sail far out from shore. She stopped and sighed deeply. She could have had an assignation if she had wanted one. But her contrary body had found nothing of that much interest. The man had been good-looking in a collegiate sort of way, but she had felt nothing.

JoAnna scuffed her toes in the sand as she started walking slowly back in the direction of her beach house. Well, at least one question had been answered—at least she now knew for sure she wasn't a nymphomaniac!

* * *

As JoAnna reached out to open her front door, it was to find that her beach house was no longer empty. Even before she had the door fully cracked, she heard Luke Morgan's deep voice raised in anger.

"Look, I don't know who the hell *you* are, but JoAnna told me I could use her telephone."

Another masculine voice snarled back: "That's easy for you to say. For all I know you could have broken in here and be in the process of carting off everything JoAnna owns!"

"In what?" Luke demanded. "My bare hands?"

JoAnna threw the door the rest of the way open, her wide eyes racing from first Luke Morgan to the smaller, more wiry frame of her middle brother.

"Peter! What are you doing here?"

Both men turned to look at her. Peter was the first to speak. "This man says he's your neighbor, Jo. Is he?"

Her eyes met the still-angry gaze of Luke Morgan. He looked at her as if she was something soiled.

"Did you miss him down on the beach, JoAnna?" he questioned nastily. "I guess he got impatient. I know I would if I were in his place."

Peter looked both indignant and confused. "What the heck's he talking about, Jo?"

JoAnna could not withdraw her gaze from Luke's. Strange little blue sparks were lighting fires in his gray-blue eyes and she was transfixed, held by a power that was stronger than her will. After a long moment Luke turned away in disgust.

"Thanks for the use of your phone . . . Jo. Maybe someday you'll let me repay you."

The door closed behind him with a restrained bang.

53

"JoAnna, I want to know just who that man is and why he was talking to you in that way." Peter had donned his most authoritarian tone of voice.

"He's . . . my new neighbor. I thought I told you about him." She was still staring at the door.

"Not that I know of, you didn't. And what did he mean by meeting me on the beach?"

JoAnna turned to face her brother, trying to coerce a smile on her stiffened lips. "He has some mistaken ideas, that's all. It's nothing to worry about."

"That look he gave you was something for me to worry about, I can tell you that!"

"Oh, don't be silly." JoAnna moved across to her sofa. "Come on, sit down and tell me why you're here."

Peter was thirty and the proud father of a son and a baby daughter. Thinking of the purpose of his visit seemed to mollify him.

"Little JoAnna's birthday is the twenty-second. I'm here to formally invite you to the party."

JoAnna smiled. Until little Anna had been born, all the Davis men seemed able to provide was sons. JoAnna had four nephews and only one niece. In her honor Peter and his wife, Jean, had named the baby after her.

"Why, of course I'll come. What time?"

"Well, we thought about six. Jean's going to do it up big—have a dinner, cake, ice cream . . . the works. Everybody's coming. Tom has that day off so he and Sally are making an early start and Sally's going to help Jean get things together."

Tom was the brother who lived in Houston.

"Sounds better and better."

"Er. . . ." Suddenly Peter looked ill at ease. "You can

54

bring a date if you like. Jean wanted me to tell you that especially."

JoAnna smiled softly, love for her brother and sister-in-law warming her heart. She placed a hand over her brother's. "No, I don't think so, Pete, but tell Jean thanks."

"Okay, but the invitation still stands. If you think of anyone you want to ask—girl friend even—just let us know."

"I will."

The two of them went on to talk of other things and it was close to noon before Peter left. JoAnna walked with him down to the drive that led to her house.

"I wish you would stay and have lunch with me." She sighed wistfully.

Peter ran a finger down her short straight nose. "Some other time I will. But today I have to see a man about a boat."

JoAnna looked up in surprise. "You're going to buy a boat? What kind?"

"Slow down—all I'm going to do is look at it. I'm not sure if I can afford it yet."

JoAnna grinned. Peter was the best money manager in the family and if he was looking at a boat and he liked it, it was as good as sold. She raised up on tiptoe and kissed her brother's tanned cheek.

"I hope it's what you want," she whispered conspiratorially.

"So do I." Peter laughed. "I've always had a secret desire to own one."

"I know." JoAnna grinned again, then, stepping back, allowed her brother to get into his late-model Chevrolet. "See you at Anna's party," she called.

Peter smiled and waved before putting the car into reverse to back out her long driveway.

JoAnna hummed to herself as she prepared her lunch. A tuna sandwich wasn't exactly an inspiring gourmet meal, but it would have to do. It was easy and simple and she didn't feel like preparing anything more complicated.

She had just cut the finished sandwich on the diagonal and was lifting the tab on a cold can of Coke when a knock sounded on her door.

Wiping her hands on a paper towel, JoAnna went to answer it, wondering if Peter had forgotten something.

"Your boyfriend leave?" Luke Morgan's eyes ran over her slender form as if looking for evidence of "primitive passion."

JoAnna smiled to herself as she thought those words. If she didn't find something to laugh about, she would cry and that wouldn't do at all. Luke seemed to have his mind made up about her. She could probably swear on a stack of Bibles that she wasn't promiscuous and still he wouldn't believe her. Neither would he believe that Peter was her brother. None of the Davis clan bore any family resemblance, each of them taking after some long-dead ancestor. It had been a longstanding joke between her parents that they must have had a different milkman each time her mother had gotten pregnant.

JoAnna looked coolly at the man standing outside her door. "If I said no, would you believe me?"

"No, because I saw him leave. I wouldn't have interrupted otherwise."

JoAnna glared at him. "What do you want?" she asked shortly.

"I had two calls to make. Your ... friend ... interrupted me before I could make the second."

"So you want to make it now," JoAnna stated flatly.

Luke nodded. "If I may. . . ." He put a tremendous amount of irony in those three words.

JoAnna opened the door and swept a beckoning hand. "Be my guest."

Luke stalked past, brushing aside her outthrust hand.

JoAnna took her time in closing the door. Luke stood at the breakfast bar where her wall telephone was located and was in the process of dialing when she moved into the kitchen.

"This is Luke," he stated gruffly into the mouthpiece when his party answered. No words of greeting, no leading up to what he wanted. "Put Terry on the line."

JoAnna pinched a piece of crust from her sandwich and placed it in her mouth. She knew it was rude to eavesdrop on someone else's conversation, but in the circumstances she didn't feel like scurrying into another room and hiding herself away. If he wanted to use her telephone, he would have to put up with her being close by.

"Terry?" he snapped after a few short seconds. "What's happening with that last load of steel?" He frowned. "It can't be late! Damn it, man, I saw to that myself before I left!"

The invisible Terry spoke for what seemed a long time. JoAnna had a picture in her mind of him sitting up in his chair like a little puppy dog with his tongue lolling out ready to jump whenever his master called. "Well, okay," Luke continued. "See that Joe Franklin hears about this. I don't want another delay like the last one we had."

The unseen Terry must have agreed. Luke hung up the telephone, then turned to meet JoAnna's fascinated gaze.

"And what's the matter with you? Have I grown two heads?"

A flicker of amusement pulled at her lips. "No, you just reinforced an opinion I had of you."

"How's that?"

"That you're a hard man."

A quizzical light entered his blue-gray eyes and his body relaxed as he leaned against the bar. "Oh? Why do you say that?"

"From listening to you. Do you always expect people to do as you say?"

"Most of the time."

"And you make snap judgments about people and situations?"

"In my line of work I have to."

"Are you always proved right?" JoAnna tilted her head to one side, a look of bland curiosity all that was allowed to show in her expression.

"Again, most of the time."

"Then that explains why you are the way you are," she answered mysteriously.

"And how is that?" A slow smile was lightening the harshness of his features.

Suddenly the smoldering anger JoAnna had been hiding started to blaze in her green eyes and her soft mouth tightened. "That you're a self-opinionated, ignorant, pig-headed . . . boor!" All pretense at friendly curiosity was shattered by her words.

Luke straightened from his leaning position as if she had struck him. All too late he realized that she had led him down this path purposely. His pale gaze began to glitter.

"So it's back to war again," he murmured softly, his eyes running slowly over her small, furious face.

"Have we ever been on any other footing?" she demanded angrily, ignoring the excited pulsating of her blood.

For a man of his size, Luke moved with tremendous ease. Almost before she knew what was happening he had come around the end of the bar and was towering over her.

"I think there's been a time or two when we've both felt something else," he growled softly, as one of his large hands reached out to tangle itself in her hair.

His words sent a whisper of panic through JoAnna's body, but she couldn't force herself to move. It was almost as if she were paralyzed. His other hand came up and his fingertips slowly began a caressing movement against the sensitive skin of her cheek and neck.

A fluttering weakness tied JoAnna's stomach in knots. She began to tremble, and almost against her own volition, her eyes fell shut and she slowly swayed forward.

Luke seized the moment with all the quickness of a bird of prey. He caught her yielding body close to his hard strength and his mouth attached itself to hers with hungry ferocity.

Quicksilver fires exploded through JoAnna's limbs, as if they were made of dry tinder. A shaking made her knees buckle as he practically lifted her off the floor.

For several mindless seconds, caught in the haze of physical desire, her thoughts centering only upon sensation, JoAnna responded with all the fervency of her nature. But when he moved, pressing her back against the wall, the hard length of him molding itself to her quivering form, she began a desperate struggle to free herself from passion's insidious hold. His hands began an exploration of her soft breasts and his lips left a trail of fire along the sensitive skin of her neck and throat. Her breath was coming in short, shallow gasps and she knew she had to break away soon or it would be too late.

With a tremendous effort JoAnna brought up her hands and pushed against his arms with all her remaining strength.

"*No!*" The cry broke from her lips.

Luke Morgan raised his head, his eyes glittering and alive with sensual feeling.

"Don't fight me, JoAnna. You know you like it," he murmured huskily.

JoAnna twisted her head from one side to the other in exaggerated denial. She caught at her quivering bottom lip with her teeth, still feeling the burning imprint of his kiss.

"No," she whispered, tears of shame and humiliation starting to build in her eyes.

"I wasn't born yesterday. You want me as much as I do you!" He emphasized his words by crushing her hips tightly against his own, making her wholly aware—as if she hadn't been—of the depth of his arousal. "You give yourself to other men, one more can't make any difference."

The insulting words tore through JoAnna as if they had been shards of glass. Her entire body stiffened from the wound.

"Let go of me!" she cried, anger and hurt lending strength to her renewed struggles against the tightness of his hold.

Slowly Luke released her, backing up a step, his pale eyes at once icy and hard, his lips a thin line of displeasure as with taut control he mastered his surging emotions.

"All right . . . you win. This time. But I promise you one thing, JoAnna Davis." His words were harsh, determined. "One day you won't be begging for me to set you free."

JoAnna turned her cheek to the wall, unable to face the harsh condemnation she knew would be in his eyes.

"Just get out of here," she whispered, her throat aching.

After several heart-stopping seconds during which his eyes seemed to burn her body wherever they touched, he turned and walked away.

JoAnna's shoulders sagged as soon as she heard the quiet closing of the door; her chin fell to meet her chest. Then the flood tide of tears she had been holding back burst the dam that had been restraining them and her body shook spasmodically as she covered her burning face with her hands.

CHAPTER FOUR

On Sunday JoAnna did not leave her house, not even when she heard the unmistakable sound of the Bronco's engine start and drive away. She had spent another restless night, cursing herself, cursing him, and all the while remembering.... Finally, sometime close to daybreak, she had fallen into a deep exhausted slumber and had not awakened until after eleven—startled into consciousness by the sound of the car engine as it shattered the quiet of her semidarkened room.

She had greeted the arrival of the new day with an agnoized groan and the beating of her fists upon her pillow. Things did not go uphill from there. Again this morning her head ached and she felt as though she had been buffeted about in a storm-tossed sea with only a small life ring to cling to.

Two aspirins helped her headache but only a determined effort, aided by a house cleaning to end all house cleanings, helped to keep her thoughts at bay. She scrubbed and polished everything that didn't move. When darkness descended once more, she fell into her bed and, for the first time in a week, slept with little or no trouble.

The next day at work Melissa took one all-encompassing glance at her pale features and worn expression and immediately asked what she was planning to do on her upcoming vacation.

JoAnna shrugged her shoulders. Several weeks ago Philip had suggested that they arrange things so that the two of them could have a short vacation together. He thought a trip to Cozumel, Mexico, would be ideal. JoAnna had tentatively agreed but was of two minds about actually going. She knew her brothers would frown upon her spending the week alone with Philip and even though she was an adult and had long been making her own decisions, their opinion mattered—especially when she was somewhat skittish of the idea herself. She had never understood why, but even while thinking herself madly in love with Philip, something had always held her back from making a final commitment. A trip away together, where they would be in each other's company constantly during the day and most of each night, might prove too much for the fragile hold JoAnna had managed to retain on her emotions, and the idea unsettled her. Now the problem was no more and she was secretly relieved. But she had given no thought to her vacation, her mind being too occupied with other things—namely Luke Morgan.

"I know!" Melissa cried. "Why don't you take a cruise?"

JoAnna smiled weakly at Melissa's enthusiasm but shook her head. "No, I don't think so, Lissa. I wouldn't want to go alone."

"But that's just what you *should* do," Melissa burst out, her blue eyes earnest. "Go by yourself—meet people—meet some nice man."

"You've been watching too much television, Lissa," JoAnna teased. "Things don't work out like that in real life."

"The heck they don't! My Aunt Sarah went on a cruise and met my Uncle Richard!"

JoAnna spun a piece of paper into her typewriter and frowned at the folder that was open on her desk. "That was a one-in-a-million thing," she murmured, her concentration wavering from what Melissa was saying.

"Well, you've got to do something to snap out of it! Honestly, ever since you broke up with Philip, you've been looking like a wreck!"

That brought JoAnna's head up with a jerk. "Well, thanks," she muttered sarcastically.

Melissa closed the folder she had been working on and had the grace to blush slightly. "Oh, you know what I mean. I had thought that new neighbor of yours might be the answer, but either he's slow off the mark or you've frozen him out. You need to *do* something, JoAnna, get away from yourself for a while! Then maybe you'll realize that getting free of Philip wasn't such a bad thing after all and certainly not worth destroying your health over."

JoAnna sat motionless as she suddenly realized just how little she had thought of Philip over the past week. In fact, she could hardly summon up a clear image of his face. He was like a hazy memory, floating into view and then quickly receding.

"JoAnna!" Melissa's impatient voice called her back to the present.

"Hmmm? What?" She shook her head.

Melissa motioned helplessly. "Have you heard *anything* that I've said? Honestly! I get so frustrated with you sometimes!"

JoAnna had to smother a smile as her friend's redheaded temperament was ready to strike sparks.

"Yes, I've heard everything you've said. And I agree. I

do need to do something to take my mind off"—she paused, only to finish up with a weak—"things. But I'm not sure what I want to do. I'm going to have to think about it."

"Why don't you go to that travel bureau down the street on your lunch break? Get some brochures. We can look them over together!"

Under Melissa's approving smile, JoAnna agreed.

"God, what I wouldn't give for a million dollars!" Melissa breathed fervently as she looked through the brochures JoAnna had brought back with her. She nibbled at her sandwich and leaned her elbows on her desk, sighing ecstatically. "I think if I were rich, I wouldn't come home for years." She raised her eyes inquiringly to JoAnna. "Have you decided where you're going to go yet?"

JoAnna grimaced. "Not yet. The travel agent tried to talk me into going to Jamaica and the Bahamas but—"

"Oh, why don't you!" Melissa fumbled with the colorful brochures until she found the one she wanted. "Just think—seven whole days of going from one exciting place to another! It's just exactly what you need."

"Look, Melissa, if I do decide to do this, I'm not doing it to meet a man!"

"I know, I know. . . ."

"But you'll never give up hope, will you?"

"You're my best friend, JoAnna," Melissa stated simply. "I want you to be as happy as I am."

After that profound statement, JoAnna mumbled that she would still have to think about it.

It was only as she was checking her calendar for an appointment for Mr. Daniels during the week ahead that she realized that little Anna's first birthday fell exactly in the middle of her vacation. Strangely the discovery was made with more relief than dismay.

"Well, it was a good dream while it lasted." She broke the news to Melissa.

"Oh, no!" Clearly Melissa was more disappointed than she, her pretty round face crumpling.

"Lissa—" JoAnna frowned, an idea forming in her mind. "Why don't *you* keep the brochures? Show them to Bill and see what he says about choosing one for your honeymoon."

At first Melissa sat there, her dark-blue eyes a blank, then she blinked suddenly and a smile of such radiance began to beam from her face that JoAnna had to hastily look away.

"Oh . . . could I? I hadn't thought about that! A cruise for a honeymoon! What could be more romantic!" She paused and giggled. "Oh, I wonder what Bill will say?"

JoAnna answered dryly, "If I know Bill, anything that makes you happy will make him happy."

Melissa smiled delightedly, then her smile faded. "But what about you? Won't you be able to get away at all?"

JoAnna lifted her shoulder dismissingly. "I may, I may not. Peter and Jean are having a big family party. I might decide to stay with them for the week."

"That's not exactly getting away. They don't live over fifteen minutes away from you at the most."

"No, but at least I wouldn't have to stay at the beach house!"

Melissa caught the thread of feeling JoAnna had let slip from her control. Since waking up this morning she had told herself that she wasn't going to allow her thoughts to dwell on Luke Morgan. It did her no good; it only upset her. But suddenly the idea of staying at the beach house all week with him just a short distance away brought back the memory of his kiss and her response to it and she panicked, the wall she had tried to build around her feelings cracking enough to let some emotion into her words.

"And why don't you want to stay at the beach house?" Melissa was instantly suspicious.

"Well . . . as you said, I don't really think it's good for me to be alone right now," she prevaricated, improvising hastily.

Immediately Melissa was all concern. "Oh, you poor thing, I know. . . ." And to take JoAnna's mind off her problems, Melissa again broke into a monologue on which of the tourist areas she thought it would be most exciting to visit, finishing each sentence with a bite of her sandwich and a glance at a glossy page while JoAnna nodded absently and got on with her work.

The next two days it rained. The sky was dreary and dark and matched JoAnna's mood with perfect precision. Of Luke Morgan she saw nothing. He might have moved away for all she knew—leaving as quietly as he had come. His house was dark at night; his car nowhere to be seen. Absurdly the thought gave her a pang.

Late Wednesday evening the rain lessened to a heavy mist and JoAnna moved restlessly about her living room, pacing the floor, her mind perversely doing what she had tried so hard to will it not to—think of Luke Morgan. Even in his absence he seemed to haunt her. Where was he? What was he doing? Would he ever come back? She moved to the window that looked across at his dark silent house and a vision of his ruggedly handsome features flashed vividly in her mind: the fine network of lines that radiated out from his eyes when he smiled, the firm yet sensual mouth, his burnished-gold tanned skin, the dark-brown hair that blazed with chestnut highlights in the sun, the hard, muscular length of him. . . . JoAnna moaned aloud and leaned her forehead against the curtain, her fingers touching the coolness of glass. His image came so clearly it could have been branded on her brain!

She stumbled down the hall and into her bedroom, and although it was barely seven thirty she changed into her nightgown. She had to do something! She had to stop herself from thinking about Luke! She switched on her bedside light and snuggled down between the smooth sheets, a copy of Stephen King's newest best-selling paperback clutched in her hands. If anything should be able to take her mind off Luke Morgan, this should!

But much to her dismay, the master of horror and suspense could not capture her attention—especially since a short time after opening the book to the first page she had heard the unmistakable sound of the Bronco's engine in the drive next door. With each sentence she read came the thought He's back! and in the end she flung the book away, having comprehended nothing of what she read.

JoAnna lay back against her pillow and closed her eyes. Almost immediately she opened them again. It was no use; she had to get up. She rolled from her bed and padded into the kitchen, thinking that a cup of hot cocoa might settle her. While she waited for the milk to heat, she paced about the living room, her hands clutching tightly to her folded arms, her mind shooting from one thought to another. He had come back! She would see him again! But should she want to see him again—knowing the effect he had on her, knowing his potent appeal to her senses? Yes! one part of her cried out, not wanting to listen to the small voice within that was screaming out a shrill warning: Leave—

get away—do what Melissa said. Put thousands of miles between herself and him.

Unconsciously JoAnna stopped her pacing at the window and pulled aside the lightweight curtain. She looked across at the neighboring beach house and saw the glow of a lamp shining through his unadorned window. Mindlessly she continued to stare at it, blindly, senselessly, unable to draw away. It was as if the light was a flame and she a moth. All sense of logic, all sense of danger, was forgotten. The rain was falling from the heavens in a slow, languid drizzle.

A movement came into the window across the way and JoAnna blinked. Then, in the space of a second, she found herself gazing at the tall, muscular form of Luke Morgan. And he was staring back at her. Only about ten yards separated the two houses and with the light behind him and the light behind her, she knew they were visible to each other. His face was in shadow, just as she knew hers would be to him.

JoAnna's body stiffened as soon as she saw him standing there and her heart rate quickly accelerated. He was such a large and imposing figure; he almost filled the window with his presence. Once again memory pushed its way forward and JoAnna experienced the feel of being held close against that hard male frame and the demanding pressure of his lips. She caught her breath. She was dressed only in a thin nylon nightgown and knew that with the light behind her, very little of her slender shape would be left to his imagination.

Her eyes darkened at the thought and she wet her lips with her tongue nervously. She knew she should move away, the prudish side of her nature telling her it was shameful to remain standing there, letting him devour her with his eyes. But she couldn't help herself.

Her breasts swelled as she remembered his experienced touch and they tautened hotly against her gown, the nipples hard and throbbing.

She couldn't move and she couldn't take her eyes away from him. His body was still, frozen—as if Michelangelo had come to earth once again and lovingly created another masterpiece from marble.

But JoAnna was sure that at this moment Luke was not feeling like something made of cold, hard stone. She knew with a certainty that he was experiencing the same feelings as she, the same wanton desires.

Slowly he lifted a hand and placed it on the window, his palm flat against the glass. Trembling from head to foot, JoAnna saw the appeal. She knew what he was doing, what he was asking. It was an action of confirmation. If she so much as lifted a finger, he would be across the distance that separated them, dragging her into his turbulent embrace, molding her soft, pliant body to his. And this time nothing—*nothing*—would stop their mutual desire from reaching its inevitable conclusion.

JoAnna swallowed tightly, her mind and body fighting a tremendous battle. Caught in the web of his attraction, she wanted to signal her acceptance, wanted more than she ever had before in her life to taste the forbidden fruit— with this man—here—now!

And yet she remained still, her hand a lump of clay at her side, her fingers cold and dead. She couldn't do it. She wanted to, but she couldn't.

Tears started to her eyes as she slowly backed away, letting the curtain fall into place.

It was then that the smell of burning milk assailed her

nostrils. She rushed into the kitchen, grasping the metal handle of the pan with her bare fingers and crying out in pain at the contact.

Milk splattered everywhere but luckily none of it splashed onto her. Her fingers were throbbing and her tears were flowing freely. She didn't know which hurt worse: the burn or the burning ache she was still experiencing deep in her soul.

Never had two days seemed so long. Both Thursday and Friday had to have contained forty-eight hours each and nothing she did seemed to turn out right. She had even snapped at Mr. Daniels when he asked for the tenth time if she was sure she wanted to take her vacation next week. As far as he was concerned, she should work fifty-two weeks a year, with maybe—maybe—Christmas day off for good behavior!

Melissa said very little and tried to keep out of her way, something that JoAnna appreciated. She couldn't have talked about what was bothering her even if she wanted to, which she didn't.

She prayed for Friday to end and when it finally did, she slumped in her chair, her nerves shooting in a thousand different directions.

All further threat of continued rain had stopped soon after she arrived at work that morning, so JoAnna carried her umbrella under her arm and walked briskly to her car, the bright sunshine hurting her tired, aching eyes. Once inside she ran a hand over her short curls and massaged the tight muscles at the back of her neck, uttering a deep sigh of partial release. At least she wouldn't have to return to the office for a week. Now, if only she could walk away from her personal problems with as much ease.

JoAnna stared blankly at the street ahead, her fingers making no attempt to place the keys in the ignition. She hated to admit it, but she was afraid. Afraid to go home—afraid to meet Luke—afraid of herself. Ever since what had happened two nights ago, she had scrupulously avoided any contact with him, the continued drizzly weather coming to her aid. From the noises she heard after arriving home until about ten o'clock at night, he had been working on the interior of his house—seemingly not the least troubled by what had happened between them and in all likelihood not shunning his windows as if they were a trap waiting to catch unwary souls.

JoAnna uttered a deep, shaking sigh. How was it possible for her to have reacted the way she had that night? She began to tremble even as she thought of it. One little movement, one small sign, had been all he had been waiting for. . . . And she had wanted to give that sign more than she had ever wanted anything in her life—even Philip! And that was what frightened her. She didn't love Luke Morgan. She barely knew him! And yet she reacted to him with an intensity that terrified her.

She should go away; she knew she should. But she couldn't miss Anna's party because not only was she the baby's namesake, she was also her godmother. Jean and Peter would never understand her deliberate avoidance of the party—especially if her plans were made *after* accepting their invitation. Unless she lied. She certainly couldn't tell them the truth!

JoAnna started her car, the engine now purring from time spent in the garage several days before. Maybe she would spend the week at Peter's. Jean might be glad of another hand to help out with the preparations for the party and to baby-sit with the children afterward. They were always urging her to come stay with them. JoAnna comforted herself with that thought all the way back to her home. She would call Peter tomorrow and make the arrangements.

A strange car was sitting in the drive that led to Luke Morgan's beach house. It was a late-model MG with bright-red paint that gleamed in the afternoon sun. JoAnna was frowning slightly as she parked her own car in her garage and began the trip up her stairs. The house next door was still, and after a quick look showed that no one was on the beach, she turned away hastily.

After preparing a supper of soup and a salad that she truly didn't want to eat, JoAnna paced restlessly across her living-room floor. She wanted to go outside and wander the beach—that always had a calming influence on her, and heaven knew she needed calming today—but she didn't want to come upon Luke and his visitor. She knew she couldn't go on avoiding him. As they were the only people living on this stretch of beach, such avoidance was virtually impossible, but she definitely didn't want a witness to that first meeting. It was going to be awkward enough.

Steeling her frayed nerves and wavering confidence, JoAnna flicked aside the curtain that faced his house and peered across carefully. Still everything was quiet; nothing moved either within the window she could see or without. Maybe no one was there! JoAnna narrowed her gaze. She hadn't seen the Bronco, and he usually kept it parked outside in his driveway. Was it possible that Luke had taken whoever had come to visit him out somewhere? And here she was, nervous as a cat, hesitant to show her nose outside her door—and all the while he wasn't even there?

JoAnna's lip curled as she thought of the amusement that would afford him if he knew. She could just see that maddening half smile pull at his attractive mouth and the mocking look that would enter his blue-gray eyes.

Tossing her head in a fine imitation of haughty disdain, JoAnna turned from the window and went into her bedroom, there to change into a rust-colored terry playsuit that complemented her coloring and left a long expanse of delicately tanned leg bare.

She tripped down her stairs, totally ignoring the house next door, her confidence strengthening with each step she took. So what if he *was* home? She was an adult! She could handle any situation that might come up. After all, nothing *had* happened. And nothing *was going* to happen! Tomorrow she would go to Peter's and while there she would at last come to her senses. Luke Morgan had cast some kind of magic spell on her, and it was up to her to break it.

Her small chin was set in fierce determination and her lively green eyes held a flash of spirit as she neared the lower steps. Then an unfamiliar voice calling her name from a distance caught her attention. She raised her head to look at the long verandah of the house next door.

The man standing there was of medium height with a husky build and he was holding himself strangely tense.

"Are you JoAnna Davis?" he asked once again, a tinge of impatience hovering on the edge of his question.

JoAnna's descent stopped and her hand gripped the rail. "Yes," she answered slowly.

The man let out a deep breath. "Well, thank God for that! I thought you must be the girl Luke was talking about but I wasn't sure."

"Luke?" JoAnna repeated, her eyes darting past the man's husky form.

"Yeah." The man watched her for a moment before adding uneasily, "Maybe you better come over here."

JoAnna frowned. "Why?"

"Well . . ." The man scratched his head, making his dark shock of hair even more unruly. "Luke's had a little accident."

After a quick intake of breath, JoAnna hurried down the few remaining stairs, her heart thumping erratically. She didn't allow herself time to examine why she was upset, but as she crossed the sand and started to mount the stairs Luke had so recently repaired, another thought occurred to her and she stopped. It could all be a trick. She didn't know this man. He could be anyone claiming to know Luke. And even if Luke was hurt, why would he be talking to someone about her?

JoAnna's emerald eyes were large and questioning as she stared up into the man's round, beefy face. Dark-brown eyes set under thick, bushy brows looked steadily back, and something she saw in them made her lose her apprehension.

"How?" she began, but he motioned for her to come up beside him. JoAnna did as he requested, a nameless dread for what he might say growing within her.

"My name is Terry Stanton. I work for Luke." The man offered his hand. JoAnna took it wordlessly. "Luke had a fall. Oh, he's not dead or anything," he hurried on as he saw her face lose some of its color. "He just may wish he was. He's got some bruised ribs and a badly sprained ankle. But it could have been worse."

JoAnna closed her eyes, not understanding the relief she felt. "How did it happen?" she finally asked.

Terry Stanton again scratched his head, an action he seemed to make when perplexed. "Well, I don't exactly know. He said something about being up on the ladder trying to scrape some of this old exterior paint off. I guess the ladder fell with him—although it's rather ironic that he'd get hurt this way when he started out in the construction business as an ironworker on buildings twenty or thirty times this tall."

JoAnna swallowed. No wonder standing on a two-story roof was nothing to him. He was accustomed to doing an aerial ballet on narrow beams high enough in the air to sometimes be completely lost in low-hanging clouds.

"He's inside." The man motioned with his head. "He's asleep now, the doctor gave him something for pain. Luke didn't want to take it, but for once he listened to me." This was said with some evidence of satisfaction.

"So why did you call me? I . . ."

Terry Stanton frowned, making his bushy eyebrows meet in the middle of his forehead. "Because Luke said you'd want to know. He said you'd take care of him. The doctor's instructions are that he has to stay off his foot for the next three days—and those ribs of his are going to give him fits. He's not going to be able to take care of himself properly for most of next week." The man looked at her expectantly but on encountering her blank gaze continued, "I can't stay. I've got to get back to Houston and the construction company. We have schedules to meet."

"But surely there's someone else?" JoAnna protested, her stomach knotting.

Terry Stanton was shaking his dark head. "Nope. Luke's pretty much of a loner. Doesn't have any family around here that I know of."

When JoAnna made no reply, a cold, disapproving note

was added to the words Terry Stanton spoke and his dark gaze was hard.

"Look, if it's that much trouble, I think I can manage to hire a nurse to come out. I'll talk to the doctor before I go. If you could just stay for about a half hour. . . . I don't want him to wake up and be alone, because knowing him, he'd try to walk around and that's the worst thing he could do right now. As it was he had to drag himself up these stairs and into the house all on his own. He was hurt sometime this morning, and I didn't get here until a couple of hours ago."

JoAnna tried to hold herself aloof. She knew she would be asking for trouble if she agreed to take care of Luke. But then, how could she refuse? Slowly her resolve began to crumble.

"No. It's all right," she whispered over a tightness in her throat. "I'll do it."

The man's face broke into a relieved smile. "Ahhh—that's better. I know Luke was counting on you." He paused to look at his watch, a thin gold affair that looked somehow incongruous on his thick wrist. "Look, I've got to go. I'm already late for an appointment." He paused again and shot JoAnna an estimating glance. "You have a job, don't you?" At her nod, he asked, "So what will you do about next week?"

JoAnna could only stare at him, feeling as if fate had stepped in and jerked her by the hand. "I'm on vacation next week," she murmured.

"Now, that is a coincidence, isn't it?" he observed cheerfully.

"It most certainly is," JoAnna agreed, wondering if somehow Luke Morgan had known.

* * *

Five minutes later she was to take back that unworthy thought. Terry Stanton had left with a swirl of sand as he hurriedly backed down the long drive and JoAnna had slowly walked through Luke's front door.

At first she was hesitant to look for him; but, after gathering sufficient courage, she discovered him asleep on his bed.

He looked so different lying there. So . . . vulnerable. And that was a word she never had thought to use to describe Luke Morgan. His dark hair was tousled, curling slightly in disarray, his skin was a paler shade of its usual bronze, and his breathing was shallow—as if it hurt to move his abused ribs even in sleep.

JoAnna turned away quickly. She didn't want to remember him in that way. It would probably come back to torment her at a time when she least wanted it to. She moved quietly back through the open door.

Once in his living room, she sank down into his only chair and marveled at the whimsy of happenstance. Just when she had planned to get away and try to forget Luke —try to break the hold he seemed to have over her—now she was going to be thrown closer to him than ever before! As hurt as he was, she was going to have to wait on him constantly. There would be very little he could do for himself, not if he was to stay off his ankle. And what about his ribs? Was he supposed to move at all? JoAnna smiled thinly. Having older brothers who had been active in sports had given her some experience, but that was mostly limited to keeping them company while they were immobile. Her mother had done most of the actual nursing. But a great deal of nursing was good common sense—something she thought she had a great deal of in the past. It was only recently that she had become less sure. Especially since meeting Luke.

For an unknown length of time JoAnna sat in silent vigil in the chair, her thoughts forced into blankness. The room was almost in darkness when Luke's voice startled her into awareness.

"JoAnna?"

Her head spun around to find him standing in the doorway to the living room, wearing only the abbreviated jeans she was growing accustomed to, a shoulder supporting his weight as he leaned heavily against the wooden frame.

JoAnna jumped to her feet. "You're not supposed to be up!" she protested.

"I did call but when no one answered, I thought I was alone."

"I'm sorry. I—"

"Did Terry leave?" he interrupted her apology.

"Yes. Now look, you're not supposed to be on that ankle!"

"I just came to get some more ice. This damn mess has melted." He held up an ice pack for JoAnna to view.

"I'll take care of that. You get back to bed," she ordered, flustered by the fact that even injured as he was, he still managed to look big and dangerous.

In the dusky light of the room, she saw the gleam of his slow smile as he drawled, "I think I'm going to need some help."

JoAnna closed her eyes momentarily. This had all the promise of becoming a terrible fiasco. She was too aware of Luke and of her own wayward emotions. There was only one thing she could do: She had to psych herself into thinking that she really was his nurse. Her mother had had a friend, a Mrs. Whiteside, who was a nurse at one of the large hospitals in Galveston. Gruff, stern, a will of iron—one look from that indomitable lady could deal with even the most self-assured male's protests. That was the attitude she would have to strive for. She would become a younger version of Mrs. Whiteside. It was the only safe way.

"Certainly," she answered briskly. If her ready agreement surprised him, he was given little time to ponder it. JoAnna was standing in front of him almost before she had finished agreeing. "Which side are your ribs hurt?" she asked, a model of efficiency.

"My right, same as my ankle." On closer inspection JoAnna could see the large expanse of reddened skin that was already beginning to darken almost in the center of his rib cage on his right side.

"All right, lean on me." Swallowing her nervousness, JoAnna moved to put an arm carefully around his waist under his right arm and waited for that arm to settle over her shoulders. She tried to ignore the warm firmness of bare skin and keep her mind on easing his discomfort. With only a moment's hesitation, Luke rested his arm over her slender shoulders, his hand curving to touch under her chin. JoAnna had to forcibly still a violent tremor.

As they moved down the hall toward his room, she could sense that his earlier challenge might not have been made totally with an ulterior motive because she could feel his large body wince occasionally as they walked.

"Does it hurt very badly?" she finally asked as he lowered his weight onto the bed. Beads of perspiration were standing out in stark relief on his forehead.

"In the old cliché, it only hurts when I breathe." He

laughed shortly, then winced again. "Lady, if you want to pay me back for anything, all you have to do is tickle me."

JoAnna smiled faintly. "That's not a very wise thing to tell a person—especially when you can't fight back."

His pale eyes ran over her face and hair as he murmured softly, "I guess I'll have to trust you then."

JoAnna met his gaze and felt herself take a step closer to the edge of the giant whirlpool that was his attraction. Hastily she drew back, straightening abruptly.

"I—I'll see about the ice." She schooled her features to belie the pounding beat of her heart.

He watched her for a moment in silent contemplation before he nodded. "That might be a good idea."

JoAnna walked from the room calmly enough, but once outside she was seized by a fine trembling. She had to hold her arms closely against her breast as she hurried down the hall, all the while castigating herself severely because Mrs. Whiteside would never have reacted to a male patient in the manner in which she just had.

CHAPTER FIVE

Before the next hour had passed, JoAnna decided that Luke would have to be moved. He was little more than existing in this empty shell of a house. The electricity was still off—he probably was planning to replace the old wiring with new—and the amenities in his kitchen consisted of an ice chest, a one-burner camp stove, a wide assortment of canned goods, a can opener, and a fire-blackened skillet.

JoAnna shook her head in disgust. She would not be able to care for him properly there. For one thing, the small amount of ice that remained would not last. And she had no intention of packing trays over from her home several times a day. Nor was she going to glide about through the night like Florence Nightingale with a lighted taper in her hand. No, he would have to be moved—and there was only one place to take him.

After making that fateful decision, JoAnna marched into Luke's bedroom. She had left the big battery-powered lantern with him after her earlier foray into nursing and now saw that he was reading a book in its high-powered light.

She flicked off the flashlight she had used to help guide her way before entering the room. With some sense of satisfaction she noted that his ankle was still propped up on the pillow she had insisted needed to be there and the ice pack was securely in place. As far as his ribs were concerned, JoAnna had learned that letting nature take its course was the doctor's only prescription.

Luke looked up inquiringly as she approached the bed, his eyes moving disturbingly over her bare legs before coming to rest on her face.

JoAnna tried to ignore that wholly masculine look and stated baldly, "We have a problem."

"Oh?" He didn't seem in the least perturbed.

JoAnna nodded. "Tomorrow we're going to have to figure out some way to move you to my place—just until you're over the worst of this."

Luke lowered the book onto his bare chest and an amused smile chased away the lines of discomfort that had settled about his mouth. "You had to qualify it—just when I thought things were beginning to look up between us," he murmured softly.

JoAnna flushed, hating the way he could melt her hard-won poise with a word or a look. "I've decided it will be much easier to take care of you there than here," she replied stiffly. "If you object—or if you think it will cause you too much pain—we won't do it."

Luke's eyes danced. "Oh, no, I have no objections. I've been trying to find a way to move in with you for the past week."

His outrageous reply stunning her, JoAnna drew in a startled breath and her green eyes flew to his—wide, disbelieving. He returned her gaze levelly, amusement at her reaction more than evident. JoAnna took refuge in anger. She replied tartly, "Don't get any ideas, Mr. Morgan. I'm only doing this because I'm stuck with you. And while we're on the subject, what *ever* made you tell that man I would take care of you?"

"I don't know. It seemed like a good idea at the time." He shrugged lightly with his good shoulder.

"Well, I wish you had had another idea! My vacation is next week—and my plans hadn't included playing nursemaid to you!"

Luke tried to look repentant but failed. "The new boyfriend going to be upset?" he suggested provokingly.

"No." JoAnna pressed her lips together.

"Were the two of you going someplace in particular?"

"No!"

"Ahh, I should have guessed. Since you like making love in the sand and surf, here is as good a place as any. There's no use spending good money to fly somewhere halfway around the world when what you need is right outside your door."

JoAnna was seething, and it was all she could do not to slap that handsome, taunting face. "I'm not going to stay here and be insulted," she warned him tightly.

"All I'm doing is telling the truth. Don't you like to hear it?" he responded innocently.

JoAnna gritted her teeth and sent him a look of total dislike before she turned on her heels and marched out of his room, her breath coming in quick, agitated spurts. She didn't stop when she came to the living room but continued on to the front door. She didn't care if he was hurt! He could get along on his own as best he could. Right now it didn't matter to her how much discomfort he experienced, because he certainly didn't mind inflicting pain on her.

She slammed the door behind her and began a quick

descent of the outside stairs, the glow from the moon above lighting her path.

She was almost to her own stairs when she heard Luke's voice calling urgently to her. She stiffened before slowly turning. He was standing on his verandah, one hand holding onto the front railing and the other pressed tightly to his hurt side, splinting it. He was bent slightly at the waist, giving in to his pain.

"JoAnna, wait! I'm sorry." His words were thick, forced. "I didn't mean for you to go."

JoAnna stared at him for another moment, then as his large body swayed slightly she began sprinting back toward his house muttering "You idiot, you idiot!" all the way, not knowing if it was to him or to herself that she was addressing these words.

Once she had her small frame next to his, giving him her support, she decided it would be ridiculous to take him back into his bedroom. They were already well on their way to her house, and since he had walked to where he was strictly on his own, surely with her help he could make it farther.

"Look, since we're this far—" she began.

"I can make it," he interrupted shortly, almost under his breath, immediately understanding her meaning. He straightened away from the railing and momentarily let his chin rest on the top of her head, his breath playing in her soft curls. "Thanks for coming back," he whispered.

JoAnna shivered convulsively and swallowed before directing gruffly, "Come on. You shouldn't be standing any longer than you have to. Hold on to me tightly."

His next words were so soft that she barely heard them. It sounded as if he said "Don't worry, I plan to," but she wasn't sure. When she glanced up at him questioningly, she was alarmed by the paleness of his skin and the deep grooves of stress that were etched at each side of his mouth. She immediately urged him to start the long hard trial that would take them to her home. She knew if his strength gave out, she would be unable to move him herself.

JoAnna directed Luke's dragging steps into her guest room. She wanted to apologize that the curtains were pink-flowered pieces of fluff and that everything there spoke of blatant femininity, but from the weight he had increasingly been placing on her shoulders, she didn't think it would make a bit of difference to him.

"Where are the pain pills the doctor prescribed for you?" she asked tensely as she helped him lower himself into a reclining position on the bed. His ankle must have been hurting terribly. She was so much smaller than he that he had been forced to support a great deal of his own weight, and she could tell from the discoloration and swelling that it was badly sprained.

"I don't want the damned things. I don't like them," he answered testily, his words coming from between tightly clamped teeth.

"Whether you like them or not is immaterial. You need them. Now, where are they?"

"You're enjoying this, aren't you?" he accused, and JoAnna, having grown up in a house that was dominated by males and the male ego, recognized the symptoms for what they were—injured pride at having to rely so heavily on a female.

"Definitely, what did you expect? You enjoy bullying people when you get the chance, don't you?"

"Just wait until I'm back to normal—"

"I'll do that. Now, where are they?" With little grace, he told her. "You stay put—I'll be right back," JoAnna warned unnecessarily, then had to smile to herself as she heard him mutter a reply under his breath that it was probably better for her not to have understood.

She located the bottle with little trouble and soon was back with a glass of water.

"Open wide," she prompted with disgusting cheer.

Luke looked at her with a jaundiced eye. "Goddamn it, woman, I'm not a baby!"

"You're acting like one."

He took the capsule from her hand and downed it before she could hand him the water. "Wouldn't you like even a little sip?"

He glared at her. "What I like doesn't seem to matter."

"Not when I'm your nurse, no."

"A real nurse would probably be less trouble," he grumbled, resting back against the pillow and grimacing.

"I can always call one."

"Never mind. Just go away—for now, I mean. These damn pills make me drunk and when I get drunk I get sleepy." He closed his eyes. She stood watching him for a moment, looking at the way his dark lashes rested against his high cheekbones. Without warning his eyes flickered open again. "You still here?"

"I'm just going," she retorted, spinning about and putting her words into action.

"JoAnna?" he called as she neared the door.

"Yes?" She paused and turned slightly.

"Thanks." He closed his eyes once again.

Quietly she closed the door behind her. Later when he was fully asleep she would come back and raise his ankle with a pillow and apply the ice pack. Right now she didn't want to press her luck.

Much to JoAnna's surprise she drifted off to sleep immediately that night. She had thought Luke's presence in her house would have kept her awake, but instead she seemed to relax fully for the first time in what seemed to be weeks.

In fact, she was so deeply asleep that at first she didn't hear the soft cursing as a chair tumbled over; but when a second noise broke the stillness of the night, she sat up in bed, her eyes wide and her heart beating like a wild thing. Was someone in her house? A burglar? Then she heard the sound of a hushed voice and remembered that Luke was there.

But what was he doing up? Quickly she swung her feet to the floor and hurried across her room.

"Luke?" she whispered expectantly. "Is that you?" she called as she tiptoed down the hallway toward his room.

"It sure as hell isn't Godzilla!" he growled, his temper smarting as he tried to right the frilly chair that he had knocked over in his attempt to leave the room.

"What are you doing up? Don't you know you're only making your ankle worse? You have *got* to stay off of it!"

"JoAnna"—Luke's voice was soft—"I'm glad you're so concerned, but I *had* to get up."

"What for?" she asked stupidly, her eyes trying to see in the dimness of the room where only the light from the moon outside permeated the darkness. Instinctively she moved closer to Luke to help balance him.

She felt him sigh even though she knew it must be painful.

"I'm a mortal man, JoAnna. I have needs, desires . . . and bodily functions."

JoAnna turned her face away so that he couldn't feel the heat of her embarrassment. "Oh," she said weakly.

"Yes, 'oh.' You do have a bathroom in this house somewhere, I suppose."

"I'm sorry—yes, it's down the hall."

"Good, that's all I needed to know." He started to limp away.

"Luke Morgan, stop right there!" JoAnna rushed forward. "You're not to put any more strain on that ankle than you absolutely have to. At least let me help you." She paused, waiting to see if he would listen. When, after a moment, he raised his right arm, she moved against him quickly to lend her strength in supporting his injured side.

The walk down the hall was short, and when they arrived at the bathroom door, Luke released his weight from her and transferred it to the door jamb. She could barely see his face but she knew he was smiling.

"That's far enough, I think. While I'm in here, why don't you fix me something to drink? I haven't had anything since breakfast this morning."

"Would you like an egg or something?" JoAnna inquired. She didn't have any idea of what time it was but somehow it didn't seem to matter.

"No, I can wait until morning. But some coffee would be nice."

JoAnna hummed softly to herself as she prepared a tray that contained a cup, sugar, cream, and a plate of cookies to take to his room. When she heard the bathroom door open, she rushed across to help him back to his bed. Then she switched on the hall light in order to locate the ice pack and took it back to the kitchen to refill while she waited for the kettle of water to come to a boil.

Taking a chance on his taste, JoAnna made the instant coffee strong—he didn't look the type who enjoyed colored water. And she was proved correct. He took it straight and from the contented sound he gave upon tasting his first sip, she knew she had done the right thing. The cookies had been a good idea too because they disappeared with surprising speed. JoAnna smiled to herself. When he was done, she took the tray back to the kitchen.

Luke was resting full length on the bed when she returned, the light from the hall casting its glow into the room. Her heart turned over when she glanced up to see him watching her as she gently lifted his foot to place it on the pillow and secure the ice pack in position. It was then, for the first time, that she became aware of the brevity of her clothing, of her thin nylon gown that did little to conceal her slender shape and of the neckline that was cut low enough in front to expose the upper half of each gently rounded swell of breast as she bent to complete her task. The intensity of his gaze caused her to straighten abruptly.

"God in heaven, you're beautiful, woman," he breathed huskily, drinking in the vision she made.

"I—I . . ." JoAnna stuttered, her entire body coming alive to suffocating awareness.

"Come here," he whispered. "Don't be afraid, I won't hurt you."

JoAnna moved as if she were a puppet and he the master of her strings. She came slowly to stand at the side of the bed, looking down into his ruggedly handsome face and into the eyes that glittered so strangely.

"Sit down beside me, JoAnna."

JoAnna lowered herself to the bed, her hip softly touching against his and feeling scorched from the close proximity. She started as his hand raised up and he smiled easily. "It's all right, I promise." JoAnna closed her eyes as delicious sparks of excitement were beginning to ignite deep within her. She held her breath waiting for what was to come next, knowing that whatever it was, she would do nothing to stop it.

Featherlike strokes on her face and neck forced her languid green eyes to open. He was trailing his fingers gently over her creamy skin, dwelling for a moment on the curve of her mouth and chin. Then his exploration widened and his fingers followed the line of her gown to her breasts, there to remain for a time, stroking the soft, sensitive skin the gown exposed but straying no farther below the white nylon.

"Beautiful," he repeated huskily. His hand moved away and JoAnna swayed slightly, suddenly bereft at the loss.

Luke caught her arm, his gaze studying her lips. "Kiss me, JoAnna, just once—kiss me. I'm in no shape for anything else. You don't have to be afraid I'll take advantage of you."

His soft, seductive voice could have persuaded her to do anything at that moment. "I'm not afraid," she whispered and ever so gently lowered her head until her lips touched the warm firmness of his.

For a moment the kiss was sweet and innocent, then the deeply banked fires that had been smoldering for far too long broke their bonds and consumed them both in a burning conflagration of mutual need. Her lips parted under the hungry ferocity of his, their breath mingling, their bodies straining together. Dizzying excitement filled JoAnna's body, leaving it weak and trembling yet intensely aware. Her thoughts were unformed, her senses awakened to only one need. . . .

All too soon it was over and he was pushing her away. "Much more of that and I won't be able to keep my promise," he stated wryly, his breathing unsteady. "Bad ribs or no bad ribs!"

JoAnna smiled shakily and ran a hand over her tumbled curls. She could still taste the feel of him on her lips, the tender skin vibrantly alive and tingling as was the rest of her.

As if unable to help himself, he reached out to touch the side of her cheek before saying gruffly, "Maybe you better go back to your room now."

"Yes. . . ." Still JoAnna hesitated, suddenly enveloped by a dazed feeling, as if somehow this had all been a dream. But when she saw the beads of perspiration that had broken out on his forehead and the drawn lines of strain that had formed at the sides of his mouth, she knew this was no dream. "Are you in much pain? I—I can give you another pill." Her words were breathless.

Luke grinned lazily. "Honey, the kind of pain I'm in right now can't be helped by pills."

JoAnna stared at him blankly for another moment before the meaning of his words became clear. Then she blushed deeply; his candor was one of the things about him that consistently disconcerted her.

JoAnna awakened the next morning feeling as if some nameless shift had taken place in her world. It was as if an enormous quake had rumbled beneath the crust of the earth yet had left everything above undisturbed. A casual observer would see no difference. Her room was still the same; the pictures on the wall were straight. The little china figurine Bob had given her for her birthday in April was still on her dresser. Everything about the day was perfectly normal. But JoAnna knew it was not.

The upheaval had been within herself. Almost with a sense of wonder she traced the path Luke had blazed the night before, the tips of her fingers moving softly over her lips and down to the beginning curves of her breasts. And there she stopped; just as he had. A simple touching and no more. JoAnna closed her eyes as a surge of remembered feeling washed over her. It had been like a dream. A beautiful dream—a dream in which they both had responded with wholehearted enthusiasm. When they kissed, she had not wanted it to end and neither had he. It had seemed so right.

JoAnna sat bolt upright in her bed. It had seemed so right. *Why* had it seemed so right? And she had even told him that she wasn't afraid! Why? Why?

Oh, God! she thought, panicking. She wasn't falling in love with the man, was she? She began to shake her head at the thought, her eyes wide with shock. No! It was impossible. She wouldn't let herself!

JoAnna threw back the bed sheet and jumped to the floor, but when she tried to walk, her knees felt like so much Jell-O, trembling in the wake of a very severe aftershock. She stumbled over to her dresser and stared at her wide-eyed reflection. She couldn't love him! She didn't even like him! It was impossible to love someone you didn't like! She blinked at the girl in the mirror, seeing the dawning realization that slowly caused the emerald eyes to darken even more. Oh, God help her, *no!* She shook her head as huge tears of misery began to drown the gemstones of her eyes. She did love him! She could deny it as many times as she wanted but the stark truth remained that it was already too late. She loved him! *She loved Luke Morgan!* And there was nothing she could do to change that fact!

The tears that had welled up in her eyes began to tumble down over her cheeks as her small hands clenched. Why? Oh, God, why? Why did she have to fall in love with him? He didn't love her. He didn't even pretend to! He wanted her and that was all. He had made no secret of it, even admitting to trying to find a way to move in with her. He thought she was a girl who passed from one man to another, and after last night, he had probably decided that he was next in line. Shattered, JoAnna moaned achingly. What was she going to do? What *could* she do?

All along she had known she was attracted to Luke; but she had never expected this! He aggravated her—infuriated her—and yet when she had thought he was badly hurt—JoAnna swallowed an agonized cry.

In comparison, what she had felt for Philip was a pale thing to what she now felt for Luke. With Philip something had always held her back from total commitment, even though she had been sorely tempted on several occasions to ignore that sole remaining thread of detachment. But with Luke all constraint was lost. If he had not been in so much discomfort from his injuries last night, she would have stayed with him. She knew that with a certainty. He had wanted it and so had she.

But if she had stayed, what would have happened afterward? Oh, it might take several weeks or several months for him to tire of her—she might even last a year. Then what? Could she take living day to day with the knowledge that their liaison might end at any time? JoAnna had watched several friends go through a similar experience and didn't relish the soul-destroying aftereffects.

If only things could be different! If only they could begin again!

She wiped the traces of tears from her cheeks and stared blankly at herself in the mirror, remembering something her mother used to say about "if only" being the two most wasteful words in the English language. "If only she had tried harder . . . if only he had had enough confidence to speak up . . ."

Slowly JoAnna moved back to her bed and sat down. Never before had her mother's words seemed so important.

After several moments of deep thought, she squared her sagging shoulders and lifted her chin. He thought she was promiscuous. And from what he had seen and experienced, he might be justified in coming to that erroneous conclusion. She had certainly done little to correct it so far. But just because an opinion had been formed didn't mean that it couldn't be changed. JoAnna's soft lips thinned into a determined line. She would have to call upon every ounce of control she possessed, but she would prove to Luke Morgan that he was wrong. Then maybe—maybe—they could start anew and he would see her in a different light—see her as someone he could love as well as desire.

CHAPTER SIX

"Good morning." JoAnna spoke briskly as she moved gracefully into Luke's room carrying a tray laden with eggs, bacon, toast, orange juice, and a cup of rich, dark coffee.

"Morning," he answered huskily, a slow, intimate smile creasing the corners of his mouth as his blue-gray eyes ran appreciatively over her dark jeans and white sleeveless blouse.

JoAnna put the tray down on a bedside table, trying to still the wayward pumping of her heart that had immediately sprung into overtime action upon seeing him lying back, propped against two pillows, a dark shadow of beard covering his cheeks and chin, giving him the dangerous air of a libertine of old. With his dark hair mussed from sleep and the lazily deceptive stillness about his large athletic form, it was easy to compare him to the pirate Jean Laffite who had long ago used the island of Galveston as a base for his nefarious operations in the Gulf of Mexico.

"Did you sleep well?" she inquired, needlessly straightening the contents of the tray before turning back to him, her features forced into calmness.

"Not particularly," he drawled meaningfully. "Did you?"

"Oh, yes," she lied unblinkingly, knowing that after leaving him in the night she had tossed restlessly on her bed until the early light of morning. "I hope you like your eggs fried," she went on, ignoring his narrowed, estimating look.

"Any way's fine with me," he answered slowly.

"Good. Now, how are we going to go about this? Do you think you'll need help? Or can you manage on your own?" She looked at him in mild inquiry, her eyes purposely devoid of any feeling.

"I think I can manage. You may have to help me sit up a little straighter though."

JoAnna hesitated, unwilling to get any nearer to him.

He smiled depreciatingly. "I'm a little sore today. I can't move about as easily as I could yesterday."

JoAnna nodded slightly, thinking that it only stood to reason. More than likely he would be extremely sore for the next few days. She bent to help him sit up. Then before she knew what was happening, his left arm had snaked out and encircled her waist. Next he tugged at her, and her unbalanced weight was brought down until she was half sitting, half lying on the bed beside him. She heard him give a grunt of pain but, mindless to anything but the need to get away, she started to struggle against the ironlike hold that shackled her close to his side.

"Stay still!" he barked out, his breath coming in short, shallow bursts.

Immediately JoAnna ceased her frantic movements, but her tongue took up the battle.

"I hope you do hurt—I hope you hurt like hell!"

Luke acknowledged her words dryly. "Lady, you're getting your wish."

"Then let go of me! That was a stupid thing to do, pulling me down like that."

"Sometimes drastic measures have to be taken to achieve an end result. I can't chase after you so I had to get you to come to me." Luke smiled slowly, then his smile faded and he asked softly, "What happened, JoAnna? What changed you?"

JoAnna stiffened, her heart pounding in her ears, the nearness of his powerful body affecting her control. "I—I don't know what you're talking about," she denied breathlessly.

The arm about her waist tightened perceptibly. "I think you do. Last night you were all warm and soft and willing . . . and this morning you march in here like a block of ice and proceed to treat me as if I'm suddenly a stranger."

"That's because you *are* a stranger! I don't know you! I don't know anything about you!"

For a moment Luke was quiet, then he answered softly, tauntingly, "What would you like to know, JoAnna?" When she didn't reply, he carried on as if she had asked an entire litany of questions. "I'm thirty-five, unmarried, I have a very successful construction company in Houston, I like to buy old houses and repair them—most of the time looking toward resale—I fly my own plane, scotch and water is my favorite drink, women are my favorite pastime, I like football over baseball . . . have I left anything out?"

JoAnna stared at him, clinging to what little composure she had left. She couldn't give in. She couldn't let that disturbing mixture of charm and determination seduce her into a reenactment of last night. She had to be strong.

"Your—your eggs are getting cold." She decided to change the subject.

"To hell with my eggs!"

He glared at her as if he would like to strangle her, then slowly the anger began to fade and a smile took its place— a devastating kind of smile that had JoAnna scrambling to fortify her already weakened defenses.

"I don't want to argue with you. We have much better things to do than argue." A slow, sensual light began to show in his gleaming eyes.

"No!" JoAnna cried. But before she could pull away, his free hand came up to press her head down to his, his lips finding her own and holding them, warm and hard and demanding. With every ounce of strength she possessed, JoAnna resisted the riotous onslaught to her senses, keeping her body stiff and unyielding and her lips tightly closed, unresponsive.

When finally he lifted his head, his eyes were glittering with suppressed fury.

"Ice—pure ice," he observed gratingly before suddenly releasing her, almost as if casting her away.

JoAnna got to her feet, her legs trembling in their effort to support her. "I-I'm going now," she whispered tightly. "Is there anything you need before . . ." Her words trailed away under the heated glance he turned on her, dislike mingling with derision in the paleness of his eyes.

"Honey, I wouldn't ask that question if I were you. You might not like the answer I give." He ignored her quickly indrawn breath and turned to pull something from the opposite bedside table. "Here, why don't you hold on to this for a few minutes. It needs to be refrozen, and I can't think of a more appropriate place than in your hands." He tossed it to her uncaringly.

JoAnna caught the now-slack ice pack in her hands and stared at it woodenly. As the intent of his words filtered into her dazed brain, her eyes blurred with tears and she raised them mutely to his, her heart speaking the words her lips would not. Then she turned and ran, not hearing the hastily uttered sound of her name.

JoAnna threw herself on her bed, sobs rising up from the depth of her despair and overflowing onto her balled-up pillow. She was so miserable she wanted to die! She should hate him—but she didn't. She should make him leave her house this minute—but she couldn't. He was hurt and she loved him, so she would take care of him. Where she had made her mistake was in thinking that he would not expect a continuation of last night. Nothing had changed for him. He still wanted her. He had no way of knowing the important discovery that had befallen her this morning—the revelation of her love for him. To him she was still the same promiscuous female he thought her to be—an easy lay. And from his very own words, women were his hobby. How could he be expected to ignore her response of last night?

Another hard sob racked JoAnna's slender body and she buried her nose further into her pillow until a soft touch on her back caused her to start. She turned tear-drenched green eyes up to meet Luke's serious expression, and she blinked in surprise.

"I'm sorry, JoAnna." He spoke quietly. "I didn't mean what I said. I guess maybe I'm unfit to live with in the morning until I have my first cup of coffee." He smiled ruefully. "Will you forgive me?"

JoAnna stared at him for a moment, loving him unbearably. She sniffed loudly and answered slowly, hardly speaking above a whisper. "I suppose I'll have to."

"That's my girl," he said with some relief. "Now, how about helping me back to that pretty little bedroom you loaned me. I really wasn't kidding when I told you I was sorer today. I'm so stiff I can hardly move."

JoAnna smiled tremulously. "Then you shouldn't have come in here."

His eyes held hers steadily. "I think I needed to."

JoAnna gazed at him for a long moment before she had to look away, the intensity of meaning in his eyes causing her blood to quicken.

The rest of the morning passed quietly. JoAnna moved her small portable television into the guest room and turned it on, wryly telling Luke that Saturday morning cartoons were stimulating to the intellect. Then, to the accompaniment of Bugs Bunny and the Road Runner, she went about the business of washing up the breakfast dishes, straightening the living room, and making her bed. That aching, hollow feeling she had experienced earlier miraculously disappeared after Luke's apology.

Later in the morning when she looked in on him, she found him asleep. The television now had an old monster movie on and she crept over to turn it off. As she crossed beside the bed again, she paused to look down at the large masculine form that so filled its narrow width, and a shaft of both pain and delight caught at her stomach. He was sleeping so peacefully, as if he had not a care in the world. His dark hair was rumpled and fell over his forehead, the slight dampness of his skin causing it to curl with more definition; and his mouth, which was usually held in firm control, was now almost as soft and vulnerable as a child's. And she wanted to kiss it . . . JoAnna quickly hurried away.

Luke slept for most of the afternoon while JoAnna did

her best not to disturb him. Restlessly she tried to read, this time choosing a paperback romance she had bought a few weeks earlier—but as before, she had trouble. Only this time her problem wasn't in concentration—it was in trying to come to grips with the heroine's problem with the hero. He was also a strong, masterly type but where he wanted to marry the heroine, she was the one who wanted her freedom. Freedom. Marriage. Luke. JoAnna put the half-finished book down with a thump and refused to analyze her thoughts any further. Marriage was something far too nebulous to even consider in the same millisecond with the name Luke.

In the end JoAnna settled to working on her shell pictures. She sat at her worktable positioned before the large glass window overlooking the Gulf and carefully glued and lacquered the subtly colored and variously sized and shaped shells onto wood. Since she had broken up with Philip and met Luke, she had not given any of her time to her hobby—her mind had been too filled with other things to do the simple task. But strangely, today it seemed to be filling a need. She didn't want to think too deeply . . . too clearly.

The sun was low in the afternoon sky when Luke finally awakened. JoAnna heard him call as she was finishing her second picture. She straightened her cramped back and stood up.

"Everything was so quiet, I thought you had gone," Luke complained when JoAnna entered his room.

"No, I was just working with my shells."

He lifted an inquiring eyebrow and she quickly explained, "Shells—I make pictures with them."

"Oh."

JoAnna moved restlessly under his gaze. He was looking at her so strangely that she wondered if he thought she was insane—that working with shells was tantamount to weaving baskets. A tiny smile pulled at her lips when she decided that maybe that was exactly the use she had put them to: something to calm fraught emotions. She quickly subdued the smile.

"Did you need something?" she asked after a few seconds had lapsed.

Luke smiled slightly, but on seeing the color rise in her cheeks as she realized the construction he could put on her words, he took pity on her by answering, "I've stiffened up again. I need you to help me get to my feet."

JoAnna looked at him suspiciously but decided he was telling the truth. He seemed to be giving more to his side than he had before.

"Are you sure you haven't hurt something inside you?" she asked when at last they had won the struggle to lift him from the bed.

"The doctor checked me out completely—x-rays and all. Said everything was all right—that I'd just be pretty sore for a few days." They were moving down the hall, his arm resting heavily on her shoulders as his free hand held his injured ribs. From what JoAnna could see of the skin on his side, the discolorations were darker than before and covered a wider area.

"I hope he knew what he was talking about," she muttered to herself, but he heard. He paused outside the bathroom door.

"*She* did. Now stop worrying. If you don't, someone might get the idea you care."

JoAnna's head jerked back but when she saw the teasing light that had crinkled the skin at the corners of his eyes, she relaxed sufficiently to retort, "Then they would be wrong, wouldn't they?"

"I don't know—you tell me."

It was the old childish game of taunt being answered with another taunt, but JoAnna knew it would be a dangerous game for her to continue playing. She shrugged her shoulders lightly and turned away.

"Say, JoAnna—could I ask a favor of you?"

JoAnna halted. "I hope you don't want me to hold you hand—because I won't!"

Luke laughed shortly, then paid for it. "Don't make me laugh. It hurts when I do."

"Serves you right," she answered with seeming heartlessness, when all the time she wanted to run to him, to try to alleviate some of his pain. "What do you want me to do?"

"Would you go next door and get my razor? And a change of clothes. No, just bring my suitcase. It's got everything I'll need in it. I've been practically living out of the damned thing since I moved in."

"Anything else?"

"No, that's all."

JoAnna hesitated, her features becoming serious. "Are you planning to take a shower? I mean . . . *can* you?" She faltered to a stop.

Luke's white teeth flashed. "I'm going to have a damn good try. I'm beginning to offend myself—God knows how you can stand to be close to me."

All the while JoAnna was running down her steps and up his, the echo of his words ran with her. Close to him! God in heaven, what she wouldn't give to be close to him! But she couldn't let herself; she had to stay in control. And each time she was close to him, her control wavered. She *had* to keep some kind of distance between them—at least until he began to see her differently.

She found his suitcase with little trouble, and after checking to see that his electric razor was inside, she scooped it up and began the journey back to her home.

"I've got it," she called through the closed door and above the sound of running water.

"Great." His voice sounded oddly muted. "Could you bring it in? I'm already in the shower."

JoAnna swallowed tightly.

"JoAnna?" he called after several long moments of silence passed.

"I-I'm here. You say you're in the shower?" Her mind was working furiously on the fact that her shower curtain was made of a heavy green plastic that could not be seen through.

Now it was his turn to hesitate, then with sarcasm heavy in his words, he answered, "I'd almost swear I am. All the evidence points to it, at any rate."

JoAnna ran a nervous hand over her short curls. What could it hurt? They would be separated by a heavy curtain. And it wasn't as if she had never been in a bathroom when a male was taking a shower. Some nights when she was young, if she hadn't marched in while one of her brothers was occupying the shower stall, she would never have had access to her toothbrush.

"All right, I'm coming in."

He muttered something but the sound of the water covered it, for which JoAnna was eternally grateful.

The room was already filling with steam when she entered and crossed to her laundry hamper. There, that should be high enough for him to reach without having to bend over, she thought as she placed the case atop it. She knew that was why he had asked her to bring the suitcase in. He had a hard time standing upright; bending was next to impossible.

She was almost out of the room when a "Oh . . . damn!" came through the curtain, the last word being changed only in deference to her presence—she knew this with a certain clarity because his tone had sounded as if he was thoroughly fed up.

"What's the matter?" she called after clearing her throat.

"I've dropped the damn soap!"

JoAnna's fast-beating heart slowed somewhat. "Well, just leave it. I'll take care of it when you're done."

Patience didn't seem to be one of Luke's virtues at any time, but especially not now. "And that's going to do me a hell of a lot of good! I'm not done yet!"

The shower curtain swept open a space and his head thrust out. "Either help me get this bar up now or find me another. I don't care which. But stop standing there as if you're some kind of offended maiden and help me."

JoAnna blinked, then went into action, pulling open a cabinet door under the basin and withdrawing a fresh bar of soap. She undid the wrapper and handed it to him.

He took it with a growled "Thanks" and a swish of the curtain.

JoAnna stood motionless, rooted to the spot. *An offended maiden!* She *was* a maiden all right—hard as that was to believe in this day and age, but offended? Lord, no! Because from the glimpse she had had of him, the rest of his body was as beautifully formed as she had thought! Granted his cut-off jeans had not left all that much to the imagination, but standing there, wet and somewhat soapy, he had still managed to look like some kind of Greek god!

And his tan had been even and smooth with no swimsuit line to mar the perfection of his taut hips.

Suddenly the room became much too hot. JoAnna fled from it as if the gates of hell had opened and the devil himself was beckoning her to come in.

It took JoAnna several long moments to pull herself together. She rested back against the cool surface of the refrigerator and waited for her heartbeat to subside to normal. Lord! Why hadn't she gone away as she had planned . . . as Melissa had tried to persuade her? Peter and Jean would have understood her missing little Anna's party. They thought she was still trying to get over Philip. Possibly they would have welcomed a vacation trip as something that would do her the world of good. Oh, why hadn't she listened!

And then she knew why. It was because even then she had been in love with Luke and only her subconscious had known. She had not wanted to leave because she didn't want to be parted from him. But God! This was *too* close.

JoAnna was almost back to normal when she heard the shower cut off. A few moments later came the sound of his electric razor as it began the tough job of grinding through his two-day-old beard.

JoAnna quickly filled the kettle with water. Maybe what she needed was a cup of tea. The English always reached for a quick cuppa whenever they needed bracing up. Maybe it would work for this American cousin.

JoAnna never had the chance to determine if tea would indeed solve her problems, for almost at the same instant as the kettle began to sing, happily signaling its readiness, an imperative knocking sounded on her front door.

Irritation mingled with puzzlement when the knocking continued unabated as she switched off the burner and began the trip across the living room. She was expecting no one today—her brothers usually called before they dropped by—and anyway, none of them would subject her to such a display of bad manners. Unless it was an emergency. . . . A frown was creasing her forehead as she hurried to turn the knob. When she saw the visitor, the frown deepened, worry changing instantly to amazement.

"Philip!"

The dazzling smile he had used earlier with such effectiveness widened. "JoAnna."

"What do you want?" she demanded ungraciously, trying to lessen the width of the door opening, her irritation returning twofold.

"I want to see you, what else?"

JoAnna stared up into the handsome face of the man she had once thought she loved and wondered how she had ever been taken in by him. He was extremely blessed by nature with good looks, but there was nothing within him to back up his attraction. His character was shallow, masking immaturity and petulance with a brash sort of arrogant assurance—and his conceit was astronomical.

"Well, *I* don't want to see you." She made a good attempt at closing the door, but he stopped her by pushing his way through.

"Now—that's just too bad, isn't it?" He smiled insolently as he moved into the room, his dark eyes laughing at her inability to keep him out.

"Get out, Philip!"

"Not until we have a little talk." He slammed the door shut behind him and leaned back against it.

"We've already had our 'little talk.' " She glared at him.

"We said everything we needed to say the last time we met."

He ignored her words, his gaze running intimately over her slender body, lingering momentarily on the agitated movement of her breast. "I've missed you, JoAnna."

"Philip, I'm warning you . . ."

He pushed away from his leaning position and closed the space between them, gathering JoAnna into his arms before she was aware of his movement.

"And I'm warning you," he breathed huskily, "I intend to have you. I've taken care of things with Alice. She's giving me a divorce."

JoAnna was fighting hard to still the revulsion she felt at being held close against him. Somehow he now reminded her of a snake, his long, lean-muscled body cold and reptilian.

"So? Why are you telling me?" she demanded harshly.

He gave her a none too gentle shake. "Because you're going to marry me—just as soon as I get my papers."

JoAnna laughed shortly, pushing against his chest with her forearms. "That's the last thing I'd ever want to do, Philip. So if you're getting rid of Alice for me, you had best go back and see if you can talk her around again. I'm sure you've had enough practice in the past. It should be a snap to you by now."

Philip's hold tightened until it hurt. "I mean to have you, JoAnna!"

"And I mean for you not! Let go of me, Philip!" She began to struggle, kicking out with her foot, uncaring if she hurt him. She landed a solid hit to his shin.

Philip cursed under his breath. "You little hellcat!" His dark eyes shone with mounting fury. "I'll show you . . . I'll show you that you still want me."

JoAnna twisted her face away as his mouth descended, causing his moist lips to slide over her cheek to her ear. His breathing was escalating rapidly, and he tightened his grip even more until it was all JoAnna could do not to cry out. But she wouldn't give him that satisfaction. She jerked and pushed and in the end was able to free her leg far enough to bend a vicious knee to his groin.

Almost immediately she was set free, her emerald eyes blazing and her breath coming in ragged gasps. Philip was doubled over in pain.

"Ahh, very good, my love. I thought for a minute I was going to have to come over there and help."

JoAnna flashed a look over to the opposite side of the room. Luke was standing there, his hard muscles rigid under his bronze tan even as he rested, seemingly lazy and relaxed in his position against the living-room door frame, a towel hitched negligently around his hips.

Philip's head jerked upright at the low amusement-tinged words.

"You!" he mouthed, still unable to straighten completely, his eyes widening at Luke's state of undress.

Luke smiled maddeningly from his superior position. JoAnna noticed he was leaning toward his hurt side and keeping it turned slightly away so that Philip could not see the dark bruise. His right ankle carried only a degree less weight than the other and the image he exuded was one of leashed and dangerously volatile power.

Philip seemed to cringe into himself and JoAnna didn't blame him.

"I seem to remember telling you once before to leave JoAnna alone," Luke remarked mildly, his pale eyes boring steadily into Philip. Philip paled and gave a hunted look toward the door. "I don't appreciate you not listening and I also don't appreciate you manhandling my woman."

JoAnna's eyes widened as she watched Luke in mesmerized fascination while he continued in a calm but deadly voice. "If—*ever*—you come near her again, I'll make you wish you'd never drawn breath in this life." He paused to lend emphasis to his words. "Now, get out . . . while I'm still in a charitable mood."

By forcing himself, Philip was able to straighten and cover the distance to the door. Once almost outside, he paused, a little of his blustery pride egging him on to ignore the danger he might face.

He turned to look nastily at JoAnna. "Well, I guess this is good-bye. It didn't take long for you to replace me. But I guess women like you give off a scent." His dark eyes moved over her insultingly before turning to Luke. "I wouldn't hang around too long, man," he confided, his features suddenly becoming ugly. "She seems to get tired of only getting it from one man after a time. She gets bored." He met JoAnna's stricken eyes with a smug smile of satisfied revenge, then turned and hurried away down the stairs—the lunging movement Luke made spurring him on his cowardly way.

The scene inside the house after he left was one of frozen immobility. JoAnna stared blindly at the now-empty doorway and Luke stood watching her.

CHAPTER SEVEN

It seemed an age before JoAnna could move. Her entire body seemed to be made of the frailest glass and if she breathed she would shatter.

Suddenly she began to tremble and tears welled up in her eyes, only to roll unheeded down over her cheeks. She felt cold—oh, so cold.

"Come on." Luke's husky voice prompted her to move. She looked up at him unseeingly. "You need to sit down." He guided her to the sofa and, after seeing her seated, moved with some difficulty into her kitchen. With remembered accuracy he found and poured out a small glass of whiskey. When he handed it to her a few moments later, he murmured, "I seem to remember doing this once before. . . ."

JoAnna sipped the warming liquid, holding the glass in both shaking hands, her teeth clattering lightly against the rim. Philip's vicious lies still rang in her ears.

"Thank you," she breathed tremulously.

"Finish it," he ordered.

JoAnna did as she was directed, life slowly coming back into her frozen limbs, numbness giving way to aching pain. How could Philip have said those things about her? Did he hate her so much? Had his monumental ego led him to believe that she would be willing to resume their relationship where it had left off before she had known of his deceit? And when she had once again rejected him, had he struck out, trying to hurt her in the only way he knew —through Luke? Luke had told him they were more than just neighbors. Then for Philip to see him there, in her house and obviously just out of the shower—had he thought Luke was living with her? Was that another reason why he had been so vindictive? Hurt pride? Did he think Luke had succeeded where he had not? Did he think that by blackening her name, he would attain some measure of revenge? JoAnna shut her eyes tightly and more tears squeezed out to follow the path of those before. What Philip didn't know was that his witness was sorely unneeded. Luke had already formed his opinion of her. And it wasn't complimentary. He already thought her to be exactly what Philip said.

JoAnna rubbed at her cheeks with the unconscious action of a child, trying to erase the evidence of her tears, her heart beating painfully in her breast.

Was it only this morning that she had discovered she loved Luke? That she had determined so hopefully that somehow she would get him to change his mind about her?

The glass was taken from her unresisting fingers.

"JoAnna—" Her name was said in a tone that bordered on impatience, as if this was not the first time she had been called.

JoAnna looked up, her emerald eyes shadowed with pain and hurt. Luke was standing across from her, the bath towel slung low on his hips, his weight eased slightly on the back of a chair. She could let her vision rise no higher than his hair-roughened chest. She drew a ragged breath.

"I want you to lie down for a while." Luke spoke softly but with firm intention.

"No. . . . I-I'm fine."

"You don't look it. You look like you might pass out any second."

"No, really. . . ."

"I'm not asking, JoAnna, I'm telling. Go rest."

Finally JoAnna raised her eyes to his. His were slightly hooded by his half-lowered lids but from the tight set to his jaw and the line of his mouth, she sensed the anger that was burning within him and looked quickly away. When she made no move to stand, unwilling to trust the steadiness of her legs, she felt the intensity of his gaze run over her small, trembling form.

"That little bastard really got to you, didn't he?" he eventually bit out.

JoAnna's head jerked back. "Philip?" she asked stupidly.

"Who else?" he returned shortly. "Your boyfriend certainly likes to play rough."

"He's not my boyfriend," JoAnna denied tightly.

"Ex then. He's just lucky he got away when he did."

JoAnna's heart was in her throat. "Why?" she asked nervously, barely able to speak.

"Let's just say I don't like his methods." He paused, then demanded: "Are you walking or do I have to carry you?"

"You couldn't!" she cried, all of a sudden remembering the reason for his being in her house. Her eyes flew to his injured side and the ankle he was partially standing on.

"Want to try me?" he taunted softly. At her flustered

look, some of the tension seemed to leave his powerful frame and he surprised her by questioning further, "What's the matter? Afraid to let *me* play nurse?"

JoAnna blinked. "N-no."

"Then—" He inclined his head toward the door.

Slowly JoAnna stood to her feet. "But . . . what about you?"

"What about me?"

"You've already been up far too long. Your ankle is going to swell again. And your side. . . . You should lie down too." Her words trailed away under his amused glance.

"Is that an invitation?" he challenged softly.

JoAnna's heart gave a strangled leap and she could find no words, her gaze unwillingly sweeping the magnificence of his intensely masculine body. He didn't seem the least concerned that he was wearing so little, but JoAnna was violently aware of it. Of the slim hips, the long length of hard-muscled legs that were gently roughened with dark, curling hairs, the one tuck in the towel that held it secure. . . .

After several havoc-filled seconds, Luke at last relented, his pale eyes searching her face, lingering on the fiery spots of vivid color on her otherwise pale cheeks.

"Go on, JoAnna, go to bed. I won't keep you company today. You've already been through enough."

JoAnna turned away in embarrassed confusion, wanting only to escape from the room. Still, as she reached the door, something stopped her and reluctantly she glanced back over her shoulder. Luke was standing in the middle of the room where she had left him, but now he was leaning more heavily on the back of the chair, lines of strain and raw discomfort evident around his mouth and deeply furrowed brow.

He met her uneasy look and a slow smile of self-derision tugged at his well-drawn mouth. With a visible effort he straightened and with the same effort JoAnna responded to his need.

Wordlessly she came to stand next to his right side. She wrapped her arm about the firm warm skin of his waist and put her fingers lightly on the muscular arm that descended to lie across her shoulders. They began to move across the floor: Luke making the effort not to lean too heavily on her fragile strength and JoAnna trying desperately not to respond to the feeling of intimacy it gave her to touch him.

The next day Luke was forced to remain in bed, getting up only when absolutely necessary. His ankle was swollen and throbbing from the prolonged usage of the day before and JoAnna insisted on reapplying the ice pack. Luke was unusually quiet that day, and on several occasions when JoAnna entered his room unannounced, she found him staring at the wall, an intent expression marring his ruggedly handsome features, as if something of great import was bothering him, abstracting him.

Monday he seemed a little less stiff and the swelling had gone down somewhat. By Tuesday JoAnna could see a marked improvement in his condition. He no longer gave preference to his side and his ankle seemed to be over the worst of its hurt even with the abuse he had heaped upon it. Privately JoAnna decided it was sheer force of will that aided in his speedy recovery. A personality like Luke's wouldn't allow him to be out of action for any longer than was absolutely necessary. Also Luke had seemed to shrug off whatever it was that had been worrying him and he began to treat her in a very lighthearted manner. But that very manner somehow perplexed her. It was something that was hard to define.

That afternoon, as she was at the sink washing lettuce for a salad to accompany their afternoon meal, Luke came into the small kitchen, seeming to make it even smaller by his presence. He reached over her shoulder, plucked a carrot from those already cleaned, and crunched into it with his strong white teeth.

JoAnna scowled at him in mock exasperation. "You're going to ruin your appetite."

Luke grinned unrepentantly. "Nope—no way."

JoAnna returned to her work. Ever since lunch he had been limping about the house, no longer content to spend any of his time in bed and she had had to accustom herself to having his lean, jeans-clad form pop up whenever she least expected it.

"You know, I'm going to miss your cooking," he suggested smoothly, a little devil of mischief in his gray-blue eyes.

JoAnna's hands paused momentarily, the water swishing over her fingers. "Oh?"

"Sure. My TV dinners don't come out nearly as tasty as yours," he teased, then ducked when she twirled around to confront him.

"TV dinners! Now listen, you, I'll have you know I haven't given you a TV dinner since you came here. I'm not exactly a gourmet chef but I have managed to keep you alive!"

"Sure and I'm grateful for it, me darlin'," he answered in a most outrageous Irish accent.

"Oh—go away or I'll hit you in your ribs," she warned, brandishing a threatening fist.

"Faith and begorra—the woman's a fiend!" he cried in mock fear and moved away from her.

JoAnna laughed outright, enjoying his company, enjoying his humor. But, as she watched him walk with a slight limp back into the living room and take up the old Agatha Christie novel he had found buried in his bedside table her green eyes clouded over and her thoughts returned to that niggle of unease she had experienced over the last two days. Something was different. It was as if there had been another nameless shift, only this time she was not the object. Luke was. And as far as she could see, his inclination was to withdraw from her. Oh, he still teased her. She had come to accept that as a part of his personality just as was his strength of character and lightning-quick danger of mood when angered. But he never . . . he never made a more personal approach. He didn't touch her if he could avoid it; and as he no longer needed her assistance to walk, no occasions arose for her to touch him. He certainly never came back with any of those replies loaded with heavy sexual overtones as he once had—not since the day after Philip's visit when he was so quiet and introspective.

JoAnna slowly turned back to the running water and shut it off, a sick feeling of helplessness in the pit of her stomach. She knew that Luke's change had something to do with Philip and his reckless condemnation of her and she also knew that, in spite of everything, she loved Luke —if anything with more intensity. And not only because of his appeal to her senses. She loved Luke himself. And nothing was going to change that.

An hour later JoAnna was in the midst of washing their

dinner dishes when Luke walked into the living room and thumped his suitcase down onto the floor.

Startled, JoAnna looked around, her eyes widening as she encountered his serious expression. All through the meal the silences between them had grown and she had dreaded what she knew was to come. It was a funny thought, if she had been in an amused state of mind, but at first she had resisted the idea of Luke moving into her home. She had been afraid of him—of herself—afraid that he might take advantage of her weakness and not want to leave once he recovered. Then in just four short days everything had changed. *She* was the one who didn't want *him* to leave. She wanted him to stay forever. And he, obviously, was intent on only one thing—evicting himself. She would laugh if she didn't feel so much like crying.

"I think I've imposed on you long enough, JoAnna," he began, his pale eyes narrowing onto her suddenly still form. "I want to thank you for all you've done for me. I know I can't begin to repay you—"

JoAnna rushed in. "You don't need to do that, Luke, I—"

A slow smile caused her heart to flip. "I think I do." He paused. "I won't insult you by offering money . . . but I want you to know that if ever you need me, for anything, I'm only a call away."

JoAnna had to swallow hard through the tears that blocked the entrance to her throat. Her eyes misted and she had to turn back to the dishes quickly, presenting a stiffened back to the man a short distance away. He seemed to be forgetting everything that had ever passed between them. It was as if she were suddenly the stranger!

"I-I'll remember, thank you."

Luke was silent for a moment, watching her. Then he

asked quietly, "Do you remember when I first moved in next door, how I once told you we either had to be great friends or bad enemies?"

"I remember," JoAnna whispered, staring down at the soapy water.

"At the time we decided to be enemies."

JoAnna didn't contradict him that it was she who had made that decision. She only nodded.

"Well, I'd like to think that our state of war is over. And you can help convince me by coming out with me tomorrow evening. I'd like to take you to dinner."

JoAnna caught her breath, a feeling of joy shooting through her. But she quickly subdued it, making her face reflect only pleasant surprise as she turned back to him.

"I think that sounds like a nice idea, Luke."

"Good." He smiled appreciatively, looking so devastatingly attractive that she wanted to fly into his arms, to feel once again the hardness of his body next to hers.

Abruptly JoAnna's features clouded. "Oh! Oh, Luke, I can't!"

His gaze sharpened. "Why?"

"Tomorrow is Wednesday, isn't it?"

He nodded once, his lips thinning slightly. "Since this is Tuesday, yes."

JoAnna groaned within herself. Anna's party! Oh, why did everything have to fall at the same time?

"I've already made another commitment. Oh, Luke, I'm sorry. Could we make it another day?" With all her heart she wanted him to understand. She would rather be with him than anyone else in the world!

A coolness seemed to enter his eyes as he shrugged. "Sure. Sometime when we're both free. It doesn't really

120

matter." He reached for his suitcase and turned toward the door.

JoAnna watched him with dismay until all at once an idea occurred to her. "Luke?" She hurried around the breakfast bar, her expression hopeful. "Would you like to come with me?"

Luke pulled up short. "My idea of a good time, JoAnna, is not playing fifth wheel to you and one of your boyfriends."

"Oh—no! No, it's not what you think!" Quickly she told him about little Anna's party. "Would you like to come? My brother and his wife told me I could bring a guest if I liked."

Luke was silent, his eyes holding hers intently. Then he seemed to relax and that slow half smile tilted his attractive mouth. "Sure—why not? But it's still not exactly me taking you out."

JoAnna retorted boldly, "Is there a reason we couldn't do that another time?" She met his gaze levelly, her green eyes bright in her oval face, and soon his smile widened.

"In the words of my grandmother, you're a brazen hussy, JoAnna Davis."

For a moment the words startled her; but at the twinkle of amusement in his eyes, she wrinkled her nose, her heart beating fast and replied, "No—I just don't want to let an opportunity to eat out slip through my fingers, that's all."

Luke laughed shortly and gave a small grimace. "Damn, I'll be glad when these ribs finally heal."

JoAnna frowned. "Are you sure—well, are you sure you should go back to being on your own? I mean. . . ." She stuttered to a stop, feeling rather than seeing his deepening amusement.

"I think it's best. I can't go on forever pretending to be an invalid."

JoAnna's eyes widened. "But you weren't pretending! Were you?"

She continued to stare at him, confusion and embarrassment uppermost in her mind as she remembered all the occasions when he might have been pretending to need help when in actuality he did not—the outstanding instance being the time he dropped the soap in the shower and she . . .

A dull red surged into JoAnna's cheeks. Had that been planned? But no, he was really hurting that day. He couldn't bend at all . . . he could barely walk.

Luke smiled enigmatically and quietly let himself out the door. JoAnna stared after him in mute perplexity.

As she lay in bed that night, staring up at the ceiling, JoAnna felt all jumpy inside. It was as if ten thousand butterflies had been set loose in her stomach and they were frantically flapping their wings demanding to be set free. Luke had asked her out! And it had been as if he was wanting to start over again on a new footing. Did that mean he had changed his mind about her? Had he seen through Philip's lies and begun to question his own hastily made conclusions?

Tomorrow he was going to meet her family. Would they like him? Almost as soon as she asked herself that question, she answered it. Of course they would! They hadn't liked Philip because they had seen through the mask he wore, something she had been too blinded to see herself; but Luke was different. He was genuine through and through. A little too straightforward at times, but her brothers would appreciate that.

* * *

The next day JoAnna was proved correct, although in the beginning she had a bad moment or two.

They were expected to arrive an hour early. Jean had called to ask if JoAnna could help set up because Sally, who had originally planned to help, had called to tell them she and Tom would be delayed in leaving Houston. JoAnna had agreed happily.

When she informed Luke, he didn't seem in any way annoyed. So it was with a sense of anticipation that she took a long soaking bath, splashed herself with a delicious-smelling after-bath cologne, and donned the burgundy silk dress that was her one indulgence in madness. It was designer made and fit as if it had been sewn especially for her, the soft, clinging lines emphasizing her slender curving shape and showing off the creaminess of her skin to perfection. JoAnna spent a little more time than was usual on her eyes, adding a touch of green shadow and darkening her already dark lashes. In the end she was satisfied with the results. She felt as if she could hold her own with anyone—even her hair had fallen into place with no more than a little coaxing.

She had given no thought as to what Luke would wear; her mind had been too busy with her own preparations. So when she saw him, she was—to put it mildly—shocked.

If she had thought him devastating in his cut-off jeans and casual clothes, he was doubly so now. He was wearing an expensive-looking dark-gray suit with a matching vest, a snowy white shirt, and a dark tie. In all he managed to look as if he were a model for a company selling just the right executive style of dress—intelligent yet rugged, strong and virile with a definite flair for danger.

At her amazed stare, Luke smiled wryly, the twinkle of amusement in his eyes belying for the moment the element of sensual danger.

"Will I do?" he prompted mockingly.

JoAnna had to clear her throat, thinking that surely her heart had lodged there!

"I should think," she finally managed. "Don't tell me you had *that* in your suitcase!"

Luke shook his head, his smile deepening at her bemused statement. "No, but Galveston does have men's clothing stores."

"Oh." JoAnna's reply was thin. God, but the Creator wasn't fair to women when He made a male of the species to look like Luke! She invited him in, then hurried to her bedroom, ostensibly to collect her purse. But once there she sat down on her bed, trying to call her clamoring senses to order. When she had succeeded to some degree she glanced at her reflection in the mirror and was unsurprised to see the excited sparkle in her green eyes and the natural glow of her skin. Why, anyone would think she was going to spend the evening with the man she loved! At the pinpoint accuracy of that description, JoAnna began to giggle softly. She was like a fifteen-year-old going out on her first date! Her palms were damp, her nerves were vibrating like the sensitive strings of a fine violin. . . . With a conspiratorial wink to the girl in the mirror, she gathered her small purse in her hand and glided from the room.

Another surprise awaited JoAnna after they walked the short distance to Luke's driveway. Instead of leading her to the Bronco, he took her instead to a low-slung silver-gray Mercedes.

JoAnna gave the sports car a comprehensive look, then

turned to glance wryly at Luke. "Don't tell me," she murmured, "there are automobile stores in Galveston too!"

Luke grinned and put his hand to her back, urging her forward.

"There are, I'm sure—but this one happens to belong to a friend of mine. I didn't want to take you to a party in my work car."

JoAnna remained silent, his warm hand on her back burning through the thin material of her dress. What he didn't know was that she would ride with him in anything, even a scooter, if he would only ask.

The drive to Peter's was accomplished quickly—too quickly for JoAnna—the lush interior of the Mercedes adding to her enjoyment of being close to Luke. And occasionally, when shifting gears, his fingers would come into light contact with her thigh and a most delicious melting feeling would surge through her body. She could have moved, it would have been a simple thing. But she didn't, holding her breath, expectantly waiting for another corner to be reached or another slowdown in traffic that would necessitate a change of gears. She pretended that she was insensitive, looking coolly at the road ahead and giving sporadic driving instructions, but in reality she was a mass of trembling awareness, thinking only of the man seated next to her.

Peter and Jean's house faced Galveston Bay and was protected somewhat from the more abrasive winds from the Gulf. They too lived in a beach house but to call something so sumptuous merely a beach house was like calling a racehorse a nag. It was a huge, rambling affair with a semimodern exterior and bilevel wood decking spreading out from the raised back verandah to make a roof over a narrow canal that led directly from the bay to the side of the house. Outdoor chairs and tables were placed on each level of the decking, and the area seemed an extension of the house—an extra two rooms with only the blue Texas sky as their ceiling.

The interior of the house also carried out the modern theme, but it was the kind of modern that was easy to live with. Bright, colorful, light, with huge green plants placed in every available space and long windows that overlooked the water. It was hard to be out of sorts in Jean and Peter's home—Jean's bubbling personality forbade it. She was several years older than JoAnna, and had short, dark hair styled close to her head and a pleasingly plump figure.

"JoAnna!" she enthused as she opened the front door. "I'm so glad you could come early—and bring your friend too." Her glance made a lightning-quick pass over Luke's face and form. The sherry-colored eyes widened, but that was the only evidence of surprise she gave. "Come in . . . come in. Peter is just putting the finishing touches to Mark. The little devil hates it, but I told him he *had* to dress up for his sister's birthday."

JoAnna smiled. If she knew Mark he would rather be grubbing about in the dirt than suffering the indignities of soap and water. To a five-year-old, there are certain priorities.

As they crossed into the huge living room, JoAnna made the necessary introductions, trying to keep her voice cool and matter-of-fact. She must have succeeded because Jean showed no undue suspicion. She, the most intuitive of the family, was the one JoAnna would have to be the most careful around—unless she wanted her secret known. And, as yet, she didn't. There was little reason.

Luke responded to Jean with his patented brand of masculine charm and she was won over the first moment. But when Peter entered several seconds later, his small son in tow, JoAnna's happy bubble almost burst. Her brother's wiry form fairly bristled when he recognized the large, dark-haired man at JoAnna's side.

"You! What are you doing here?" he demanded.

Jean looked at her husband as if he had suddenly gone mad. "Peter?" she questioned, a hand rising to her throat.

Peter ignored her and turned to JoAnna for an explanation.

"Pete, this is Luke Morgan. You've already met, remember?" Obviously he did remember and just as obviously he remembered how rude Luke had been to both himself and JoAnna.

"I remember" was Peter's uncompromising reply. He glared at the taller man aggressively.

"Luke, this is my brother, Peter Davis." Hastily JoAnna hurried with the introduction.

If she had been unsettled by Peter's demanding look, it was only a preview of the one given her by Luke. A little flare of anger ignited in the depths of his pale eyes. It was as if he was blaming her for not telling him before that the man he thought to be one of her boyfriends was, in fact, her brother. But she couldn't help it; he had been so hateful that day—jumping to conclusions about everything. Her chin rose a degree, her eyes silently speaking her thoughts.

After a long moment, Luke conceded the small battle and turned back to Peter. "Now I can see why you were so anxious to protect JoAnna," he murmured, a smile beginning to dawn on his well-drawn mouth.

"Will someone please tell me what's going on?" Jean

complained, looking from one man to the other. "I'm beginning to feel as if I've come into a play in the middle of the second act!"

JoAnna hurried into the breach. "It was just a little misunderstanding, Jean. Peter came to visit me one day and found the house unlocked. I wasn't there but Luke was. He had asked to borrow my telephone. Peter thought he was a thief. It's simply a case of mistaken identity."

Jean still looked slightly confused but nodded her head all the same. Anything to get her husband back to his normal easy-going self!

"So everything is explained then." She smiled brightly from Luke to Peter, and neither proved resistant to her persuasion.

Slowly Peter relaxed his militant stance and after a breathless pause held out his hand. "As the saying goes, any friend of my sister's. . . ."

Luke smiled slightly and accepted the handshake. The tension seemed to melt from the air.

Huge sherry-colored eyes gazed solemnly from one man to the next. Both men looked like giants from his small stature—especially the one standing beside his Aunt JoAnna. Mark tugged on his father's hand. "Daddy, when can I go play?"

Peter glanced down at his for once neatly turned out son and suggested, "How would you like to look at the boat instead? We'll collect your sister and then show Mr. . . ."

"Morgan—Luke Morgan," Luke supplied.

"Mr. Morgan our new boat. That will give the ladies time to get things ready for the party without having us be in the way." The last was said more to Luke than Mark but Mark agreed readily—he would agree to almost anything that would get him outside.

The boat must have given the two men an opportunity to get to know one another better, because when JoAnna took time to peek out one of the rear windows, she saw they had come back onto the decking. Luke was sitting with little Anna perched on his knee and Peter was leaning relaxed against the railing, talking animatedly yet all the while keeping an eagle eye on young Mark's activities.

"That's quite a man you have there, Jo." Jean had come up behind her and followed the direction of her gaze. "Where did you meet him?"

"He's my new neighbor," JoAnna answered with as much offhand nonchalance as she was able. Seeing Luke sitting there with the baby on his lap was doing strange things to her equilibrium.

Jean lifted a delicately curved eyebrow. "Some neighbor! Is there something special between you two?"

JoAnna tried to keep her voice even. "I've only known him a few weeks."

"So?"

JoAnna turned in exasperation. "So nothing! Don't you think we should set the table now?"

"No—we have plenty of time. I'm more interested in what you have to say."

"Well, I'm not talking!" JoAnna smiled to take the sting out of her reply.

"Oh, yes you are, darling, but not necessarily with words."

"You're a hopeless case, Jean."

"No, not really." Jean smiled sweetly. "I'm just a romantic. Now, why don't you go see if the men need help with the children? Peter promised to keep them out of our way while we worked but I know he's probably beginning to regret it. Mark looks as if he's up to his usual mischief and Anna is shamelessly monopolizing your friend. Everything's under control here. We can finish the little that's left later. I just want to run a brush through my hair and I'll be right with you."

JoAnna slowly made her way outside. The sun was lowering in the sky and the wind had slackened. A few seagulls flew close by, curious as to what the humans were doing, then arced away, giving their raucous opinion.

Luke saw JoAnna first, his pale eyes running appreciatively over the silk dress and the way it clung to her slender figure as she walked. A faint smile touched his lips.

Peter was still talking about boats, but he paused when he followed Luke's gaze.

"Oh, hi, Jo. Are you finished in there?"

JoAnna smiled teasingly. "No, but we thought the two of you might need to be rescued." She bent down to her niece. "And how is our little birthday girl? I haven't gotten to kiss you yet, sweetheart." She smiled softly at Luke and lifted the small cherub from his knee, hugging the warm little body close to her breast.

Anna waved her arms happily and chortled something that sounded like "Nanna play!"

JoAnna laughed and observed to her brother, "I think she knows a dozen new words each time I see her."

Peter grinned. "She takes after Jean in the talking department. She never shuts up."

Jean, coming onto the deck at this time, questioned innocently, "Did I hear my name mentioned?"

Peter held out his arm for his wife to stand close to him,

his eyes dancing with warm humor. "I don't know, did you?"

Jean looked at him suspiciously. "If I didn't know you better, Peter Davis, I'd divorce you."

JoAnna enjoyed the light banter, knowing that as far as marriages go, Jean and Peter's was solid. She only hoped that one day, if she married, she would be as happy.

Luke's voice broke into her thoughts. "I don't like to tell on a fellow male but I believe you should take a look at your son." He pointed in the direction of the lower deck where Mark, the irrepressible, had found something of interest in a potted plant and was in the process of upending it, the dirt filtering down over his shirt, pants, and shoes.

Jean groaned in dismay. "Oh, no!"

Peter hurried over to the now alert boy who was trying to stuff the plant back into the pot upside down.

"Oh, no you don't, son. It's too late for that."

At that moment JoAnna's younger brother, Tom, and his wife, Sally, mounted the steps leading onto the decking from the ground below.

"I thought I heard voices back here," Tom was saying, "and we wanted to take a look at that boat we've heard so much about. Hey, what happened to the plant?"

Tom was looking humorously at the bedraggled plant Peter was placing on the deck railing.

"I'll give you one guess," his brother replied dryly.

Tom took in his nephew's crestfallen expression and dirt-riddled clothing and grinned. "Well, Sally, take a good look. In eight months' time, we'll probably have one just like him."

Stunned silence greeted the announcement. Then everyone began talking at once. "Oh, Sally, when did you find out?" "You're pregnant!" "Is that why you were late getting here?"

Luke stood quietly, watching as the family gathered around the happy couple.

Sally, a tall, slim girl of twenty-five, had married Tom six years before, the year he graduated from college. She smiled shyly. "Well, we hadn't planned on announcing it quite like this, but yes, I am pregnant. We found out for sure this afternoon."

Tom beamed proudly.

After that the party turned into a dual celebration. Everyone moved into the house, and with the arrival of Bob and his three sons, drinks were passed around to toast the honorees. Sally, already conscious of the new life growing within her, decided to do her toasting as the children did, with a glass of ginger ale.

The murmur of conversation was buzzing softly around them when Bob sat back in his chair and narrowed his eyes at Luke. He had been introduced to him earlier but in the commotion of being greeted and told Tom and Sally's news, this was the first time he had really been able to look at the man. A frown creased his brow. "Don't I know you from somewhere?"

Luke raised his gaze from the amber liquid he had been slowly swirling in his glass, his eyes noncommittal. "I've been thinking that same thing myself."

Bob rubbed at the deep cleft in his chin. At thirty-six he was the oldest of the Davis clan. He had been divorced for the past three years and seemed content with his lot—he and his ex-wife actively sharing the responsibility of raising their sons.

"I know!" He remembered suddenly. "We met at a

party John Masters gave last fall. You own the construction company that won that big bid he let out. Right?"

Luke nodded, sipping his scotch and water, letting his gaze casually wander over the talking groups of people.

Bob sat quietly for another moment before abruptly stiffening as if a thought had struck him that he didn't enjoy. His blue eyes shifted to JoAnna, who was sitting at Luke's side, but he looked quickly away when she arched her brow in silent question.

After that Bob seemed very quiet, scarcely taking part in the various conversations directed his way during dinner. Though his thoughts seemed to be turned inward, several times JoAnna felt his eyes fasten on her, only to glance away quickly when she glanced up.

Luke was at his urbane best, impressing her family strongly and favorably. He seemed able to find a topic of interest with each of them, and that included the children —from the youngest, Anna, who made a statement of her femininity by preferring to sit either close to or on Luke's knee, to Bob's older boys, aged fifteen, twelve, and ten.

But it was unusual for Bob to be quiet for so long, so when JoAnna saw him leave the living room to walk alone on the deck, she excused herself from Sally and Jean's talk of babies and followed. As she passed the small group of males of which Luke was now a part, she heard that Peter was still expounding on the merits of his boat. Luke glanced up, sensing her presence, and for several long moments JoAnna couldn't pull her eyes away. The gray-blue intensity of his gaze acted like a magnet, a message flickering indiscernibly in their depths. It was only the indignant protests of little Anna, who had come toddling up to lean against Luke's leg and instead ricocheted off to land on the floor with a bump and a howl, that drew his attention and allowed JoAnna to move away.

Her heart was thumping madly as she closed the door behind her, and she had to take several gasps of nighttime air in order to calm herself. What had that look meant? What had he been trying to tell her?

"Jo?" Bob was looking at her in concern.

JoAnna forced herself to give a wobbly smile.

"You okay?" he asked, examining her closely.

JoAnna nodded her head, stilling the trembling of her limbs by sheer force of will. She moved over to the railing and leaned against it, looking out over the moonlit bay, her fingers curving over the smooth wood, appreciating its steadiness.

Bob came to stand next to her, also remaining still and looking out over the bay.

Slowly JoAnna became aware that Bob had switched his gaze to her profile, the intensity of his look drawing her troubled attention. "Bob?" she questioned breathlessly.

"How involved are you with that man inside, Jo?" The softly spoken words broke through his restraint.

JoAnna closed her eyes, knowing with a sense of inevitability that her brother's sudden withdrawal concerned something he knew about Luke.

With a great effort she spoke calmly. "Why are you asking?" *God! Was Luke married too?* the thought was screamed in her head. Philip had lied to her—had Luke as well?

"Because I don't want to see you hurt," Bob replied tersely.

JoAnna's heart felt as if it were going to burst, it was pumping so rapidly. She felt slightly lightheaded. "And what makes you think I'll be hurt?" she murmured.

Bob heaved a great sigh and ran a weary hand over the back of his neck before leaning his forearms on the rail.

"Because of the kind of man he is. He eats little girls like you for breakfast." He grimaced slightly at his weak joke.

JoAnna faced him bravely. "Is he married?" she asked quietly. She had never told her family of Philip's wife.

Bob laughed shortly. "No—not that I know of. He's not the type that marries." JoAnna breathed an invisible sigh of relief. "But he's still trouble. Don't get involved too deeply with him, Jo."

Was loving him getting involved too deeply? JoAnna's lips trembled, but she stilled them almost immediately and the next moment lifted her head.

"I'm not a little girl anymore, Bob. I'm twenty-five. I know that some men like to play their little game and then leave." She paused for breath. "And don't tell me you haven't done that a few times yourself. You're nice-looking, single—and you're not any more of a monk than the next man."

Bob straightened and a muscle jerked in his jaw but he refused to look away. "No, I won't tell you that. But I'm not quite as . . . as savage . . . in my dealings with women as Luke Morgan. His reputation in Houston is none too savory. Smart men hide their daughters—if their daughters let them. Last time I saw him, he was making a big play for John Masters's daughter. John wasn't pleased but his daughter sure was." Bob shook his head ruefully. "The man seems to have a fatal attraction for women."

Tell me about it, JoAnna thought achingly. She knew Bob was only doing what he thought was best, warning her, but he wasn't telling her anything that she didn't already know—that she hadn't already learned firsthand.

"I realize what you're trying to say, Bob, and I appreciate it." Her rounded chin lifted. "But I have to live my own life . . . make my own mistakes. I may be one of those unlucky people who are always attracted to people who hurt them. I don't know." She shrugged her slim shoulders. "I suppose I'll just have to find out."

Bob's mouth tightened as he listened to her speak. "That's a tough way to live, honey. I know—because I've been there."

JoAnna swayed forward to place her lips against his hard cheek, moved by the loneliness behind his words.

"Maybe it runs in the family," she whispered, "at least for the two of us."

"God, I hope not!" Bob quickly denied, his arm coming up to encircle his sister's narrow waist, gripping it tightly.

JoAnna leaned her forehead against his shoulder. Hoping for him . . . hoping for her. "So do I, Bob," she murmured softly, "So do I. . . ."

CHAPTER EIGHT

JoAnna was deep in thought as she sat in the plush bucket seat of the Mercedes. It was not until the car made a sharp turn into a lighted parking area that she roused herself enough to look outside.

"What are we doing here?" she asked blankly, viewing the familiar sight.

"I felt like a ferry ride. Do you mind?"

"I—no . . ." JoAnna replied, nonplussed, as Luke expertly maneuvered the sports car into a parking place. She chanced a glance at his hard profile, then quickly looked away again.

"We may have to wait awhile," he warned, leaning back in his seat and easing his long legs into a more comfortable position.

JoAnna clasped her hands over her purse, her back remaining stiff. He looked so big and vital sitting there. Did he know how confused she felt? How disconcerted she had been when, after returning from her talk with Bob, he had treated her with such bland indifference, making her wonder if she had dreamed that intense, burning look?

"I don't mind," she replied, her green eyes fastened onto the building the ferry service used as an office. As she knew from previous visits, the building's lower section was open to the public as a comfort station containing restrooms, cold-drink machines, and maps displayed under glass with brief tourist information. She felt Luke's pale gaze come to rest on the curve of her cheek and her heart began to thump painfully.

He watched her steadily for several long moments before he turned away, his gaze fixing instead on the dark water that separated the island from the Bolivar Peninsula on the mainland.

The soft lapping of waves against the bulkhead was the only sound that intruded on the silence within the car until Luke surprised her by murmuring, "My grandmother used to bring me here when I was a boy. We would ride back and forth for hours, watching the ships come in and out of port."

"Your grandmother?" she repeated, raising her eyes. He had mentioned her once before. "Did she live on the island?"

"No—she had a place on Bolivar."

"Had?"

"She's dead now."

"Oh." JoAnna could think of nothing more to say. This was the first time Luke had spoken about his past and there was so much she wanted to know—but she couldn't make her mind function.

While she was racking her brain and mentally cursing its useless density, the shrill blast of a whistle signaled the arrival of the ferry.

It took a number of minutes for the boat to dock as it jockeyed for position between the huge wooden pilings that guided it to a safe and accurate landing. Almost as soon as the metal landing gate was secured in place, the crew began the job of directing the onboard cars in their exit, emptying first one side, then another.

Once that process was almost completed, Luke reached over to open JoAnna's door. "You ready?"

JoAnna nodded mutely, aware of the arm that was pressing lightly against her breast. Luke's pale eyes held her own but were carefully devoid of any emotion.

JoAnna shivered slightly in the brisk breeze as she waited for Luke to lock the car, but she knew the reaction of sensitive nerve ends was not all due to the air's dampness.

As they walked toward the entry ramp provided for those who preferred not to take their car on the ferry, JoAnna rushed into speech. "Peter and I used to come here at least once a week during summer vacation when I was small. Sometimes we'd spend the entire day riding. We got to know a few of the captains quite well."

Luke took her arm as one of the crew motioned for them to come on board. They hurried across a break in the line of traffic and through a doorway. Then they climbed the narrow stairs that led to the upper deck and went on through to the open observation area that faced the direction they would be traveling.

"I never did," Luke stated. At JoAnna's questioning look, he explained more fully. "Meet any of the captains. I always wanted to, though."

JoAnna tipped her head in inquiry. "Why didn't you?"

Luke shrugged. "Too shy, I guess."

JoAnna gave a low, incredulous laugh. "You? Shy?"

Luke smiled slowly and leaned his elbows against the metal railing. "I changed a lot as I grew up."

JoAnna looked at him with wide eyes, at the thick vitality of his dark hair, at the confidence that was stamped on his rugged features. Now, if *that* wasn't an understatement!

It seemed to be a long time before the waiting cars were loaded and the strong engines began their surge away from the dock. But finally they were underway.

Lights twinkled from the shoreline and the faraway lights of ships anchored offshore mingled with those of oil rigs and marker buoys.

The wind increased dramatically as soon as they were running at full power. Luke looked at JoAnna and at her tightly clenched fingers on the rail. "Would you rather go inside?" He spoke close to her ear in order not to have to shout and motioned to the enclosed area behind them with his hand.

JoAnna shook her head emphatically no. It had been at least a year since she had been on the ferry and she hadn't realized how much she had missed it. It was a part of her childhood that she would never outgrow.

Another small group of people came to stand on the deck beside them and exchanged friendly smiles.

"I always thought the best place to stand was in front— by the gate, right where the water kicks up." Luke spoke to her again.

JoAnna nodded, a happy feeling of pleasure beginning to fill her. "Me too," she returned. "Peter and I would get drenched sometimes. By the end of the day we looked as if we had been swimming with our clothes on and let them dry on our backs—repeatedly."

They were quiet for a few moments and the people who were next to them drifted away. All at once JoAnna shivered, the wind harsh on her exposed skin.

Luke noticed her tremor and asked, "Cold?"

JoAnna nodded, a twinge of excitement shooting

through her as he moved close and put his arm around her shoulders, pulling her against his warm, hard body.

"Would you rather have my coat?"

Silly man! Did he honestly think she would prefer his coat to him? He didn't press for an answer when she didn't reply.

The trip to Bolivar didn't last nearly long enough. Soon the ferry was jockeying for position and the cars that had loaded on the island were starting their engines, ready to continue their land-bound journey.

While they waited for the transfer of cars, Luke took JoAnna inside and sat beside her on a narrow bench. The distinctive smells of metal and grease and fuel made her nose twitch in fond remembrance. JoAnna sat quietly, the shoulder and side that had been pressed to Luke feeling quite naked. She glanced at him from beneath her lashes and saw a distant expression on his hard features. His physical presence was with her but his mind was many miles away. She searched for a question that would prompt his return and this time was successful.

"Did you live with your grandmother when you were a boy, Luke?"

"Hmmm? What?" He frowned at her.

JoAnna had to clear her throat after that almost irritated look. "Your grandmother . . . did you live with her?"

Luke shifted position, folding his strong arms across his chest. He took a long time before answering. "For about five years I did. Up until the time she died." He seemed unwilling to say anything further and JoAnna floundered about in her mind for another question. But Luke surprised her by going on. "My father had died a few years earlier and my mother . . . well, she couldn't cope." JoAnna remained tensely silent. "When I was about twelve, she ran off with one of the men she met at a bar and I came to live with my grandmother."

JoAnna wanted to say something but she couldn't. Her life had been so different from his. Stable, secure. Never had she experienced the kind of trauma Luke had been forced to face—at least not until the loss of her parents; and then, thankfully, she had been old enough to deal with it.

Amusement pulled at Luke's firm lips. "Hey, don't look so tragic! It all happened a long time ago!"

JoAnna raised a troubled face to his. "But you were so young," she whispered.

Luke's gaze held her own for what seemed endless seconds. When he spoke his voice was noticeably harder. "Contrary to popular belief, the young survive. They're the best survivors around."

A haze of tears welled up in JoAnna's eyes in spite of her effort to stop them.

Luke saw the tears and stiffened. "I don't need your pity, JoAnna," he grated harshly, his pale eyes cold. "I've never needed anyone's pity!"

JoAnna tried to control her churning emotions, but the only thought that repeated itself in her brain was that even though a child might survive, he would never forget. Now some of Luke's more puzzling aspects of character were beginning to fall into place. His father had deserted him through death; his mother through choice. His father's desertion couldn't be helped, but his mother's.... And at twelve, just when a young boy was beginning to form his attitude toward women. Was that why Luke had never married? Why he was so ready to ascribe to her the behavior of his mother? Did he feel that way about all women?

Is that why he used them and then discarded them before they could reject him—unknowing that few ever would?

"I don't pity you, Luke—" JoAnna began huskily.

"Then why the tears?" he demanded harshly. "If it's not pity, then what is it?"

JoAnna could only stare at him, the emerald green of her eyes darkening with intensely felt emotion. What could she answer? Could she tell him that it was love—love for the young boy who had been so terribly hurt; love for the man who had turned his back on the scars?

At her continued silence, Luke snorted derisively. "I had thought better of you, JoAnna. I didn't think you were the type to go all sentimental—and especially for someone you barely know."

JoAnna felt as if she had been struck. Barely know! The pain splintered through her. She lifted her chin, a proud anger slowly beginning to build. "And I had thought better of you, Luke Morgan!" she snapped. "If you didn't want me to feel sorry for you, why did you tell me?"

Luke's gaze became glacial, the gray of his eyes like ice. "God knows! A momentary loss of good sense is the only excuse I can think of!"

JoAnna's chin lifted higher, a tinge of angry color in her cheeks. She turned to look pointedly out the window. "If you feel that way, maybe it would be best if I stayed in here on the trip back."

"Are you telling me, in that sweet little way of yours, to get lost, JoAnna?" His voice was low and dangerous, and a shiver ran up JoAnna's spine.

She straightened her shoulders. "Exactly."

The waves of displeasure vibrating from the large body beside her almost battered JoAnna with a physical force, and she sensed rather than saw the clenching and unclenching of his fists. Then he was on his feet and striding away, barely contained anger evident in every step.

JoAnna stared after him, her heart pounding unsteadily in her breast.

The trip back to Galveston seemed to take forever as JoAnna sat in a tight ball of misery on the hard bench. When the ride was over, Luke came back for her, his face a granite mask, his eyes cool. As he walked beside her to the car, not a single word was exchanged.

JoAnna sat rigid in her seat. She didn't want things to be like this between them but could do nothing to break the strained silence.

When the car turned into the driveway to Luke's beach house, she knew that something would have to be said and said quickly. And from the look of Luke's still-tight lips and stiffly held shoulders, he was not the one who would speak first. When he cut the engine, she reached out to touch his arm, chancing his anger.

"Luke . . . Luke, I'm sorry. I'm sorry I said what I did. I didn't mean—"

To her consternation Luke didn't wait for her to finish. Instead he jerked open his door. Paying no attention to her hand, he moved away, slamming the door to behind him.

JoAnna was left stunned by his rudeness. As she watched him stride down the path to the beach, the full moon showing his abrupt movements when he took off his jacket and swung it over his shoulder, her anger began to burn. How dare he leave her like that! As if she hadn't been talking! And not only talking—apologizing! And to make matters worse, their disagreement was not wholly of her making! She opened her door to run after him, but her flimsy high-heeled sandals began slipping in the loose sand

and finally she had to stop to take them off. Once that was done, she hurried forward, catching up with him as he began to walk along the water's edge. She stopped before him, her hands on her slim hips and her green eyes blazing with temper as she demanded: "All right! What more do you want! I've apologized!"

Forced to halt his stride, Luke looked down at her, the rugged lines of his face causing her soul to twist. "Don't ask stupid questions, JoAnna," he grated, brushing past her.

JoAnna moved to keep up with him. "Why not?" she insisted, wanting to keep some line of communication open with him, oblivious to the danger she was fast approaching.

"Because I'm tired of playing games."

"Well, how do you think I feel?" she questioned shortly, almost panting in her effort to keep up with his ground-covering pace, her desperation making her do the unforgivable. "What happened, Luke?" she taunted. "Didn't you like being told to get lost? You're usually the one to end a relationship, aren't you? Is this the first time a girl's ever gotten in ahead of you?"

All at once Luke halted, and JoAnna almost fell trying to stop her forward speed. Uncaring of the damage to the fine material, he dropped his jacket onto the damp sand and reached out to grasp her upper arms, his fingers biting into the tender flesh. The glitter of a thousand tiny stars seemed to be in his eyes.

"We've never *had* a relationship, JoAnna," he ground out, his anger no longer controlled. "But I'm more than willing to start one if you are." He jerked her close to his hard body in one smooth motion. "Would you like to hear some pretty words?" he muttered, his voice poignant with emotion. "You look beautiful tonight—more beautiful than a woman should be allowed to be. You've got the kind of body that keeps a man awake at night thinking about and eyes that can haunt his every waking moment. You're beautiful and desirable and available. And you want me as much as I want you. We both *know* that."

JoAnna tried to pull away, frightened by the hard passion she had unleashed.

"Luke—" she began, only to be interrupted by his harshly worded:

"Why didn't you listen to your brother, JoAnna? He warned you to stay away from me!"

JoAnna gulped, unable to answer.

Luke shook her slightly, bitterly. "I knew as soon as he recognized me he was going to warn you. Why didn't you listen?"

The breeze from the Gulf played with the tendrils of JoAnna's short curls and breathed a soft caress on her cheek. Her eyes were dark and mysterious as she stared up at him, beginning to be caught in the tug of emotion that was as old as time itself.

"Luke..." she breathed his name, but this time there was a difference. She was aching for him—needing him. For much too long she had been away from him—away from his touch. She didn't care any longer if he was angry, if he had cause, if she had cause. She didn't care that she should resist. She only knew one thing: that she needed him as much as she did life itself! "I'm not a child, Luke..." she whispered.

"Do you think I don't know that!" he demanded angrily, then his hands loosened their bruising grip and began to caress her arms, moving over her skin lightly, sensually.

His touch sent tremors through JoAnna, the sweetness

of it more than she could bear. Without conscious thought she moved closer, arching her body to his.

She heard his swift intake of breath before she was crushed against him, her breasts flattened to his chest and the heat of his hard body burning through the material of his vest and shirt. The heady scent of spicy aftershave mingled with the masculine essence of his body and acted as an aphrodisiac to JoAnna's heightened senses. Then he was kissing her and his kisses were like a drug: The more she tasted, the more she craved. Almost before she realized what was happening, the zip to her dress was undone and he was sliding the soft burgundy silk from her shoulders and letting it rest on the sand beside his jacket.

JoAnna gasped with pleasure as his head lowered and buried itself in the valley between her breasts, the plunging neckline of her slip making his journey an easy one.

"You're beautiful," he rasped unsteadily as he raised his head, his thumbs massaging the hardened nipples that strained against his touch.

As he bent to run his lips over the sensitive skin of her neck, a flood of feeling caused JoAnna's knees to buckle. Soon they were lying on the sand, his tongue parting and then probing the fresh moistness of her mouth, inviting an answering response. In the past JoAnna had found kissing so intimately to be slightly repellent—not even Philip had caused her to change her mind—but with Luke it was another way of being a part of him and her arousal heightened, just as she felt the answering harshness of his breathing and the hardness of his body as he lay against her when she tentatively returned the thrusting movement.

"I want you, JoAnna Davis," he murmured, "I've wanted you for a long time." He slipped the straps from her shoulders, exposing the creamy swells of her breasts to the moonlight and his view. "God, how I want you!" He stripped off his vest and tie and began to loosen his shirt buttons, but JoAnna stopped him. Slowly, deliberately, with her eyes holding the burning look of his, she undid the buttons one by one, pausing in her course to rub the soft tangle of body hair that grew on his chest and trailed down onto his flat stomach.

"You're a witch," he groaned when she was done, his hands running the length of her body, moving over her curving hips and along her silken thighs. "A witch!"

JoAnna was trembling uncontrollably, letting instinct guide her, her breasts tingling from the intimate contact with his naked chest. She loved him; she wanted him; what was happening between them was beautiful!

At first she didn't understand the soft murmuring coming from beside her ear. Then, as the words became clear, she wished that she had not.

". . . make you forget . . . I'll make you forget them all. You belong to me, JoAnna, only me. I'll never let you leave me—never let you go. . . ."

At one and the same time, the words thrilled and horrified her. For a moment love and desire fought with shock. But in the end shock won, and immediately her body grew still.

"What?" she whispered, hoping desperately that she had heard wrong. "What did you say?"

Luke, feeling her sudden withdrawal, lifted his head, a puzzled frown beginning to form on his brow. "What is it?" he inquired huskily, his eyes on the swollen loveliness of her lips.

"I want to know what you just said," she whispered unsteadily.

Luke remained motionless above her. "When?"

"Just now." JoAnna tried to cover her breasts.

Luke watched her movements, his eyes narrowing into slits as he responded dryly, "I believe I said I would never let you go—or words to that effect."

"No. Before that."

The lines on his forehead deepened as the tension between them mounted. "What is this, a quiz?"

JoAnna flushed. "No, I—"

He interrupted harshly. "No, you've just decided to change your mind! Well, I'm sorry, sweetheart, but you're not going to get away with that this time. You can blow hot and cold with other men—but not with me. Not here . . . not now!"

He caught her hand and pulled what little material she had been able to gather away from her breasts, his eyes glittering into her own challengingly. Then his gaze lowered and JoAnna began to struggle as his head descended, his lips instantly searching for and finding their target. Her breasts swelled in response to the hot insistence of his lips and a surge of desire almost destroyed her resistance. But the echo of his words allowed her to gain a measure of control and she cried, "Stop it, Luke!"

"Why?" he demanded harshly, lifting his head. "Isn't this part of the game? Aren't I playing it right? What does it do for you, JoAnna? Does it give you some extra thrill to make a man want to rape you?"

Stung to the quick, JoAnna cried out, "No! No, it doesn't!"

As if purposely trying to hurt her, he continued. "The setting is right. We're here on the beach—your favorite place—and we're all alone. Come on, I'll play along . . . just like all your other lovers."

"I've never *had* any lovers!" JoAnna protested wildly, willing him to believe.

Luke laughed shortly, transferring his grip to her wrists and forcing them above her head, his weight crushing her deeper into the sand. "Tell me another one, Jo."

All at once JoAnna could take no more. Huge tears of accumulated hurt welled up in her eyes and began to run into her hairline. She loved this man! She loved him with everything that was in her—and he thought she was no better than a tramp!

With a harshly muttered imprecation, Luke loosened her wrists and rolled away as racking sobs began to shake her body. When she was free, JoAnna covered her ravaged face with her hands and turned onto her side in the sand, uncaring that her slip was lodged about her waist or that Luke was standing above her, looking down.

"I told you I was tired of games, JoAnna," he said flatly as he bent to retrieve his clothing from the sand. "Games are for children to play. When, and if, you ever do grow up—come see me. I still consider our business together unfinished."

With that he turned and walked away, leaving JoAnna huddled on the sand, curled in a fetal position and her eyes tightly shut, trying to forget the sound of his harsh voice.

CHAPTER NINE

Everything seemed so simple when you were a child. Black was black and white was white and gray was only some obscure color that somehow displeased you. But as you grew older, gray became the predominant color. Everything was shaded in gray and there were no more absolutes.

Was coming to that conclusion part of the act of maturing? Did everyone have to face that discovery before they were truly adult? Because if that was so, JoAnna decided, she had finally attained adulthood at the age of twenty-five. She sat on her small sofa, her legs curled under her and her nightgown tucked under her knees, staring across at the window that faced Luke's beach house.

It would be so easy to hate him—hate him for what he believed, for what he had done. But she couldn't. She still loved him and it didn't matter that he had abused her, insulted her. She just knew that she ached to see him again. And her reasons were all mixed up in that nebulous gray area.

He had accused her of being adolescent. But she knew she was not. Not any longer. He had seen to that. He had wrung what was left of her childhood away from her with the sure touch of his masterful hand and had left her to make that discovery without so much as a backward glance.

He was such a complicated person! Would she ever truly understand him? Would she ever get the chance? And how were they going to survive as such close neighbors? They could scarcely ignore one another.

A tiny ray of hope shone through the clouds that had descended on JoAnna's spirit. This was Thursday; there were still four days left of her vacation. Maybe if she went to him—talked with him—perhaps he would listen, would believe her if she told him that he was wrong in what he thought about her. There had been times when they had talked quietly, even laughed together, and never had she felt so close to him as she had last night, until. . . .

JoAnna jumped to her feet and hurried into her bedroom. She turned her eyes away from the pile of clothing huddled in the corner, her beautiful burgundy silk dress and its matching slip, not wanting to recall Luke's cutting words. They had reverberated through her brain during most of the dark hours until dawn and she knew them by heart.

She pulled on a pair of white slacks and a pink cotton gauze blouse, ran a brush through her hair, and added a little lipstick. Her eyes looked smudged but she could do little about it. That had come from hours of crying and very little sleep. JoAnna lifted her chin proudly. Well, no more. She would be strong. It was going to take courage but things could no longer continue as they had. She would do whatever it would take to convince him.

But JoAnna's plans hit a snag. On her way up his stairs, she saw that the Mercedes was no longer in the drive. This discovery shook her momentarily, but she decided that Luke had probably brought the car back to his friend before she had awakened. As she had had so little rest during the night, she had slept late into the morning. Next she found that not only was the Mercedes missing—so was Luke. And her forced feeling of optimism took a decided turn for the worse.

It did not improve over the next two days. Luke was gone, having disappeared as quietly as he had appeared. And if it weren't for the evidence of her battered emotions and the partially rebuilt beach house next door, she would have doubted his very existence. JoAnna sank deeply into a fit of the doldrums.

Sunday morning she stirred herself enough to dress and attend the nondenominational services of a small church that was located among a cluster of houses several miles from her home. She drove back afterward a little lighter in spirits, until she saw the empty beach house that was a neighbor to her own. Had he gone away for good?

JoAnna was thawing a hamburger patty for her noontime meal when the purr of a car's engine broke the sound of the gently lapping waves against the shore. It was coming from the driveway next door. Luke had come back! Quickly JoAnna hurried over to her window and, pulling aside the curtain, peered outside, her pulse pounding and her palms cold and damp. It was silly to react this way, but she had begun to think that she would never see him again.

When she saw Luke's tall, muscular form slowly come into view, her heart leaped in gladness. Then almost as quickly it froze, for a little behind him, her arm hooked proprietarily through his, was the most striking redhead JoAnna had ever seen. The woman looked like a model— all sleek and smooth and very expensive. And she was laughing up into Luke's smiling face as if she were quite accustomed to doing so. JoAnna felt as if an invisible knife had been plunged into her chest and twisted. She expelled a deep breath and for long moments forgot to take another. She watched the two people cross the short distance to the stairs and saw the woman as she seemed to be remarking on the amount of progress Luke had made on the beach house. She was holding onto his arm—clinging almost—and Luke was accepting it, looking down at her as he answered, although he didn't have to look down far. The woman was extremely tall, the top of her head almost reaching his chin.

JoAnna could not move away from the window. She knew she should but she didn't seem capable of making herself. She had never really expected Luke not to have other women friends, but somehow she had put the thought from her mind. Now it rushed over her like a tidal wave and the depth of her jealousy almost staggered her. Luke had been away for three days—had he spent all of that time with this woman?

JoAnna swallowed tightly as she watched them begin to mount the stairs. Luke allowed the woman to proceed him, then just after he took the first step himself, he paused and turned slowly, his piercing gaze seeking and finding JoAnna's still form as if he had known that she would be there. Time seemed to stand still during the few seconds he stared across at her, his ruggedly handsome features showing no emotion; then he turned away, followed the woman up to his verandah, and after producing a key, ushered her into his home without another backward glance.

For a few moments JoAnna remained as if thunderstruck. Finally, with a cry of humiliated pain, she tore herself away from the window, realizing that she should have moved away before. She should never have let him see her standing there like a puppy in a pet-store window! To make the picture complete, she should have pressed her nose against the glass and panted! JoAnna began to tremble, anger with herself warring with anger at Luke. What was he trying to prove? And she knew from that intent look that he had been trying to prove something. Was he showing her the kind of sophisticated woman who usually received his attention? Was this his way of showing her that he was more than capable of attracting other women—as if she didn't already know that? Any woman with a speck of warm blood in her veins would find Luke attractive. But did he have to rub it in so?

JoAnna went back to her meat patty. It was not completely thawed but she tossed it into the skillet anyway. The way she felt right now, she didn't care about anything. She would eat it raw if need be. She was not going to let thinking about Luke Morgan destroy her or ruin any more of her vacation! And she was going to start by eating her lunch—even if it choked her!

JoAnna kept to her determination. After lunch she took a book outside and pulled up a chair, stationing herself on the verandah even though Luke and his guest were outside lying on the beach, the woman wearing a minuscule bikini that left absolutely nothing to the imagination and Luke in a pair of tight-fitting black swim trunks that exposed most of his powerful physique.

JoAnna glanced at them sourly before bending her nose to her book. That she comprehended not a word was not the point. Periodically she turned a page—just in case Luke should look up at her again. She had to prove something to him too—if she was going to keep any pride about her, that was. She knew it was slowly slicing her heart into tiny pieces to see him stretched out beside that long, lissome body—the woman had placed their towels so closely together that a hair wouldn't fit between—but he didn't know it and he never would. Not by her actions.

For at least an hour JoAnna stayed outside, her gaze drawn with increasing frequency to the couple on the sand. At first they seemed only to be interested in getting a better tan, each turning over several times in order to better distribute the rays of the sun; then in the last few minutes, things had begun to change. JoAnna saw the woman start to rub the hard muscles of Luke's shoulders, her fingers straying teasingly up into his hair and down his neck. JoAnna wiggled uncomfortably in her chair. When Luke turned over lazily and grasped the woman about her waist, pulling her to him, JoAnna could take it no longer. She fled inside. She didn't care if Luke saw her leaving or not. She could not sit there and calmly watch him make love to another woman! It was asking too much!

JoAnna paced restlessly across the living-room floor, her nails biting into the flesh of her hands as she held them in tightly clasped fists, her mind dwelling on what was probably happening right now on the beach. That woman certainly wouldn't stop Luke if he wanted to make love to her—she had practically been attached to him from the first instant they arrived. And it was not as if this was the first time. Three days of making love were probably behind them, if not more. To them this was like adding a cherry to finish off the dessert!

The ringing of the telephone broke into JoAnna's tortured thoughts. She reached for it as if it were a lifeline, her voice coming cracked and low.

"JoAnna?" It was Peter. "Is that you?"

JoAnna cleared her tight throat. "It's me, Pete."

"Are you all right? You sound a little . . . funny."

"I'm fine," she lied bracingly, willing herself not to break down. Before tears had seemed a long way away, her anger carrying her through; but with Peter's familiar voice sounding so—so caring, all at once she wanted to howl.

Peter seemed to hesitate a moment, as if deciding whether she was telling the truth; then, after seemingly coming to a decision, he exclaimed lightly, "Well, good—because I'm going to make you an offer you're not going to be able to refuse."

JoAnna's smile was wobbly but she forced herself to respond in kind. It was the only way to convince her brother that all was well with her. "Oh? What kind of offer? Have you found the way to turn lead into gold and you're going to give me a full partnership?"

"Better than that: I'm going to give you a ride in the latest acquisition of the Peter Davis family. It'll just be the two of us; the kids have come down with some kind of virus and Jean doesn't think it would be a good idea for them to be out on the water. But you won't mind that, will you?"

"And miss a chance to be with one of my favorite brothers?"

"I always knew you liked me."

"Don't get a swelled head. What time do you want me to be there?"

"Whenever you can. I've already had her out once this morning." He paused before asking tentatively, "You're not tied up or anything, are you?"

JoAnna thought of the long afternoon spent in her own company with only images of the couple next door to fill her time. "Not at all," she answered tightly.

"Then come on over. The boat's all gassed up and ready to go!"

"I'll be there in two shakes."

JoAnna did not pause to check her appearance. She was still wearing the jeans and green pullover she had changed into after attending church, and she knew that they were still fresh. And anyway, she didn't want to meet the eyes of the girl in the mirror again—especially right now. She had been avoiding that confrontation more and more as the days went by, not wanting to see the haunted green eyes and the certain thinning of her face. The best-laid plans of mice and men . . . she didn't know who had first uttered that quotation, but it seemed painfully appropriate to her situation with Luke. Somehow she could not see herself going over to talk with him anywhere in the near future. It would be too humiliating.

She found her purse and hurried out the door, keeping her eyes firmly turned away from the beach. When she got into her car, her breath was coming fast as if she had been running—which she had been, mentally if not physically. As she backed up, one quick glance showed that it was the Mercedes that was sitting in Luke's driveway. Either he had not given it back to his friend or else the friend was that woman. Somehow that thought was especially painful.

Peter was waiting in front of his house. "Jean just got the kids down for a nap. Come on around back," he advised.

JoAnna followed her brother to the rear of the house where the boat was sitting in the small alcove that was part of the long canal leading to the bay.

"I think I knew I was going to get a boat when we

bought this place," Peter was saying, looking proudly at his new purchase: a gleaming seventeen-foot inboard/outdrive, built of cream-colored Fiberglas with royal-blue pinstriping down its sides and a royal-blue interior. "Well, what do you think of her? You didn't get much of a chance to see her the other day."

For a moment JoAnna could only stare blankly at the boat. So much had happened over the past few days, the party seemed to have taken place months ago.

"I think she's simply beautiful, Pete," she finally managed.

"If you hadn't said that, I wouldn't have let you on board," he teased.

"Don't listen to him, Jo." Jean was coming down the side steps from the upper deck. "He would shanghai the devil himself if he thought it would give him an excuse to play with his new toy." She gave her husband an exasperated look. "Honestly! Men!"

Peter laughed outright. "You're probably right." He jumped onto the boat and raised the lid of a concealed storage compartment. "Darn it! I forgot the cold drinks!" He glanced up at Jean and smiled. "I don't suppose I could convince you to go get them."

Jean smiled back sweetly. "You suppose right. I was up half the night with sick children. That's why I look such a wreck now."

JoAnna's eyes skimmed her sister-in-law's pretty features. The only thing that was different about her was that her hair was slightly disarranged.

"You're right," Peter agreed readily. "I forgot about that."

"You forgot because you slept through it all."

Peter grimaced. "I think I'd better leave before all my

sins are told. Make yourself at home, Jo—I won't be long."

The two women watched as husband and brother bounded up the stairs two at a time. Jean shook her head and smiled.

"Do men *ever* grow up?"

JoAnna looked away, pretending a sudden interest in a marsh bird some distance from them. She shrugged her shoulders as a reply, then jumped when a gentle hand touched her arm.

"Is something the matter, Jo? You don't look as if you feel very well either."

Leave it to Jean to spot trouble with only a second's glance! JoAnna shrugged again. Tension was like a tight ball inside her. Instead of being lessened by her distance from Luke, it seemed to have increased. Every time she wasn't actively turning her mind away from Luke, her thoughts seemed to home in on him as though she were a receiver and he a powerful transmitter.

"If you want to talk about it later . . . or anytime," Jean was continuing, "remember that Peter and I are here and that we love you."

JoAnna's shoulders were stiff in their effort to remain erect. She wanted to turn to Jean and sob her troubles away as a child would. But crying would do no good, and neither would involving anyone else. Luke was a problem only she could solve. She nodded her head jerkily. "I'll remember. . . ."

The sound of Peter's steps as he hurried across the deck above and then sprinted down the stairs drowned out the whisper of her words.

"Ready to go?" he demanded.

Jean turned to him. "Peter, I don't believe JoAnna

really feels like doing this. Why don't you put it off until another day—sometime next week maybe? And anyway, the weather forecast doesn't sound too promising. Some kind of front is supposed to move in this evening."

"Jo?" Peter halted and looked questioningly at JoAnna's pale profile.

JoAnna turned slowly, her features carefully under control. She couldn't go back home, and if she stayed here any longer, she would soon be blubbering about her hurt. So there was only one thing left to do, and perhaps being out on the water would help soothe her. "I'm fine . . . really. I just have a small headache."

"And a spin would do that good," her brother answered promptly. "Jean, you're a worrywart." A tender smile took the edge from his words. "A lovable worrywart, but all the same a worrywart."

Jean refused to be dissuaded by his teasing. "I still don't think you should go. I told you that earlier."

Peter sighed. "Look, we'll be fine. The bad weather isn't supposed to move in until tonight and we'll be back hours before that. We're just going for a short ride. I'm not planning on making a run to Mexico!"

"I know that—" Jean answered worriedly.

"Then stop fussing. Maybe what Jo needs is to get away for a while."

Jean looked at JoAnna's green eyes, which looked so large and bruised in her small face. "Maybe you're right," she agreed slowly. "Just don't be gone too long!"

"We won't. Come on, Jo. Let's go before she can find another reason to stop us." Peter leaned across and kissed Jean soundly. "Go see about your little chicks, mother hen. JoAnna and I can take care of ourselves."

As they pulled away from the mouth of the canal and

entered the open bay, JoAnna looked back to see that Jean was still standing beside the boat stall. Tentatively she raised a hand to wave, and after a moment Jean returned the salute. JoAnna frowned slightly. She had never experienced that flash of awareness some people call clairvoyance but just now, looking back at Jean, a sense of foreboding had washed over her. She turned to glance at Peter. The sun was shining brightly on his tanned face and the wind was blowing his dark hair. At that moment he gave her a boyish grin, including her in his happiness. She smiled back, although hers was a trifle subdued. No, it was silly, she decided, dismissing the thought. What she sensed was just a holdover from Jean's own uneasiness. There was nothing for her to worry about. Peter knew what he was doing.

"Damn it! I don't understand how this could happen! This is a brand-new boat!" Peter was once again trying to start the engine that had refused to function for the past half hour. "Oh, *hell!*" He finally threw himself onto the seat beside JoAnna. JoAnna wisely remained silent. "It was running perfectly when I zipped around the bay this morning—and now, out here, it decides to quit." Peter looked at JoAnna worriedly. "Sorry, kid, I didn't mean for this to happen."

JoAnna put a soothing hand on her brother's arm. "You couldn't know, Peter."

Peter placed his hand over hers, pressing it to his flesh. "No—"

"So don't blame yourself!"

Peter shrugged, his face a study of disgust. "Jean's going to be worried when we don't get back."

JoAnna stared at the great expanse of water between

them and the unseen shore. What could she say? Jean *would* be worried.

"If we only had a radio . . ." she murmured, more to herself than to him.

Peter sat forward, his elbows resting on his knees. "I have one scheduled to be installed next week. Fat lot of good that's doing us now though."

A silence descended upon them. JoAnna broke it by asking hesitantly, "What are we going to do, Pete?"

Peter sighed deeply. "Wait. What else *can* we do?"

Being an islander, JoAnna knew the dangers that could face a small boat adrift on the open Gulf. Her childhood had been sprinkled with newspaper and television accounts of people reported missing. Some had been rescued; others never were found, or if they were, it was because their bodies washed ashore days later. She shuddered at the thought.

A flash in the sky caused her to look up. Oh, Lord, as if they didn't have enough trouble! The mass of dark clouds seemed to be growing steadily—the bad weather Jean had spoken of was approaching more quickly than forecast. Small-craft warnings were probably being issued by now, telling boat owners not to put out and advising those already in the Gulf and bay to return to port.

But what could she and Peter do? With the storm's approach, the wind was steadily pushing them farther out to sea and the shallow anchor could not reach purchase. They were being swept farther away with each moment!

JoAnna swallowed tightly. Jean's premonition had been right and so had her small niggle of uneasiness. But blame could not be put on Peter. He had stayed within sight of shore, just running the boat about, enjoying showing JoAnna how well she handled. Then without warning the engine had started to misbehave and finally stop. Peter had worked with it, trying to juggle the insides, hoping by some chance he might find the trouble—but he didn't.

Peter was still leaning forward. "Jean will call the Coast Guard if we don't show up soon." He spoke quietly.

"Yes."

Peter got to his feet and reached into a compartment. "Here—I think we better put these on. I don't want to frighten you, Jo, but we're going to have to ride out that storm and it might get rough." He handed her a life preserver.

Without a word JoAnna complied. "Do you have anything we can signal someone with . . . just in case?"

He bent to the compartment again. "I know I should have prepared more for something like this. Here, a flashlight . . . that's all I have."

JoAnna smiled through her apprehension. "It will have to do."

Peter looked at her for several long seconds. "Thanks, Jo."

JoAnna frowned. "Whatever for?"

"For not making a scene—but I should have known. You never have been one to panic."

In the hours that followed, JoAnna was hard pressed to live up to Peter's claim. More than once as the small boat was lifted and cruelly thrown about by the angry waves, she wanted to cry out in fear. Several times she was sure they would capsize—then, miraculously, they righted. The wind drove rain down on them unmercifully, soaking their clothing, their hair, their skin. Lightning flashed, putting on a spectacular display, and the thunder hurt their ears. When the storm finally passed, night set in, the hardest night JoAnna had ever spent. Wet, exhausted, miserable—the three words did little to express the true state of their discomfort. They huddled in wet seats as best they could, trying to outdo each other in optimistic pep talks.

Finally the morning sun began to peep over the horizon. JoAnna's throat was sore from talking, and she stretched, hating the feel of being unable to change into dry clothes.

"Shouldn't be much longer," Peter said bracingly.

"No. How far do you think we've drifted?"

Peter sat up and looked about. "Can't tell. At least the wind has stopped pushing us. We could be heading back toward Galveston for all I know."

JoAnna looked at her brother appraisingly. "Do you really believe that?"

Peter would not meet her eyes. "The Coast Guard is out looking for us. They probably have been since last night. It won't be much longer," he added stubbornly.

The sun had moved high in the sky and Peter was to repeat those words many more times before the whirling blades of a helicopter could be heard from the distance.

Immediately Peter was on his feet. "Damn, I wish that flashlight hadn't fallen overboard. We're probably nothing more than a speck on the water!" He began to wave his hands over his head in wide arcs.

JoAnna sat for a moment, her mind working. "I have something!" she cried, jumping toward the compartment where her purse was stored. "A mirror!"

"Great!" Peter grinned broadly, all the while keeping up his waving movements. "Start signaling!"

JoAnna found the sun with the surface of the mirror and then angled it in the direction of the helicopter, moving it so that the reflected light made a pulsating flash.

Within minutes the helicopter was hovering above them, the men inside reassuringly visible.

"Anyone hurt?" came the deep sound of a man's voice as it was greatly magnified by a loud hailer.

Peter shook his head no with much exaggeration, the loud sound of the helicopter drowning out any attempt at normal speech.

"What's your problem?"

Again Peter resorted to pantomime. He pointed to the rear of the boat and then made a slashing motion across his throat with his finger.

The men in the helicopter spoke to each other, then the man with the hailer called down to them once again.

"We've reported your location to our nearest boat. They'll be here shortly. All right?"

Peter waved agreement, then turned to hug JoAnna as the helicopter lifted off. "See," he shouted above the noise, "I told you they would find us!"

JoAnna was never to forget the kindness exhibited by the men of the Coast Guard crew. Seeing that she and Peter were damp and miserable, they transferred them to the larger vessel and hooked a tow to Peter's boat. Once safely inside, they were wrapped in light blankets and offered hot cups of coffee. Never had coffee tasted so welcome. They were assured that Jean had been called and given the news of their rescue and that they were unhurt. She would be waiting for them at the Coast Guard station.

After a trip that was to have been a brief outing, they finally docked back in port over twenty-four hours later. In all the misery JoAnna had given little thought to her job, but as they left the boat she overheard an ensign mention that it was Monday. Oh, Lord! Poor Melissa and

Mr. Daniels. Did they think she had forgotten to come back from her week's vacation? And what of Luke?

Several times her mind had turned to thoughts of him—especially when things were at their worst and she was afraid they were going to be swept into the sea—but along with those thoughts were ones of him with the redhead, a reminder of why she was on Peter's boat in the first place. Was Luke even aware that she was not at the beach house? Or had he been too busy to care? Bitterness had been added to her misery.

As they moved up the wooden walkway toward the station offices, JoAnna began to feel decidedly shaky. She had had nothing to eat since noon the day before, and her stomach was growling loudly in protest. She looked back for her brother. He was following, talking with the mechanic on board the Coast Guard vessel, who had told him he would take a look at the smaller boat's engine. Peter looked slightly bedraggled but by the animation of his gestures, hunger and fatigue had not yet caught up with him.

A door opened some distance ahead of them and Jean came running out. She was unable to wait a moment longer. She ran past JoAnna as if she didn't see her and launched herself into Peter's arms. JoAnna watched, her spirit aching. What she wouldn't give to have someone welcome her survival like that—no, not someone—Luke.

She glanced around as more voices could be heard coming from the direction of the open door. Her green eyes widened as she saw Tom and Bob. They came toward her smiling and speaking huskily, patting her on the back and finally taking turns gathering her into their arms.

"You two scared us silly, my girl," Bob was saying. "What in God's name happened?"

"Tom?" JoAnna could not take it in. "Bob? What are you doing here?"

The two brothers looked at each other wryly. "The girl's been missing since yesterday afternoon and she doesn't think we should be worried! Come inside, Jo, you need to sit down. You're looking a little pale. Did that crazy person have anything edible on board?" Bob motioned toward his younger brother, who was still trying to disengage himself from his wife's hold.

JoAnna shook her head slowly.

"Lord, you must be starving then." He pushed her sideways until Tom was carrying most of her weight on his arm. "Let me go rescue Peter from Jean and we'll get you two back to his house. All the kids are there—Sally stayed with them."

"We held a regular vigil," Tom murmured into her ear teasingly before adding soberly, "But it wasn't funny yesterday or today either for that matter."

JoAnna started to walk, her head now feeling more than a little funny. She had to concentrate on putting one foot in front of the other. Tom was talking but his words seemed to run together and sound fuzzy.

They were almost to the door when something drew JoAnna's attention. She had to blink her eyes several times before they would focus, then her breath caught somewhere in her throat and her heart leaped with gladness. Luke! Luke was here! He *had* come!

But rather than running to her as Jean had Peter, he was standing there, leaning against the door frame. His arms were folded across his chest, an unreadable expression was on his face, and his eyes were as cold and hard as an arctic day. JoAnna stared uncomprehendingly at him for a moment before slowly crumpling to the ground.

CHAPTER TEN

JoAnna regained consciousness to the sound of raised voices.

"My God, what happened?" "JoAnna?" "She's fainted!" "Somebody help me pick her up—she's limp as a dishrag!"

JoAnna tried to protest, to tell them that she was all right, but her voice wouldn't come. Then she felt steel-hard muscles lift her up from the ground and cradle her against a rock-hard chest.

She felt motion and the dimness of a building.

"Where can I lay her?" She recognized the voice as belonging to Luke.

"Over there, sir" came the reply from an unfamiliar voice.

She was slowly lowered onto a hard vinyl-covered couch and a pillow was placed under her feet.

With a great effort, JoAnna opened her eyes and blinked at the concerned faces hovering in a circle above her. Tom and Bob were pale. Peter looked as if their experience was fast catching up with him, and if Jean had not been supporting him, he would be next in line for the couch.

Their faces gave way to another one and soon Luke was squatting down beside the couch, lifting her head and helping her to take a small sip of water from the cup in his hand. All the while JoAnna could not tear her eyes away from his face. Where before he had been hard and cold, with as much emotion as a statue, now he held her gently and there was a curiously strained look on his handsome features.

"Are you all right, JoAnna?" Bob's voice coming from a distance demanded her attention.

"Yes. I-I'm fine," she whispered, staring up at her brother, a dazed look still in her green eyes.

"Like hell you are!" he replied sternly. "You've got a good case of delayed shock, and both you and Peter should be seen by a doctor."

Sister and brother answered in unison. "No!"

Peter shifted his weight onto the back of the couch. He smiled wanly. "We're just tired, Bob, that's all. Let's don't make a bigger production out of this than need be. Jo probably fainted because she's hungry. I know I am. And we didn't have any sleep at all last night."

"I'm fine, Bob, really. As Peter says, I fainted because . . . because. . . ." Her voice petered out, knowing that seeing Luke standing there so emotionless when she so desperately needed his comfort had tipped the scale of balance on her already unsteady progress. She glanced at Luke, then away again quickly.

Bob ran a hand over the back of his neck revealing his indecision.

Surprisingly it was Jean who agreed. "Peter's right. Look at her, Bob, she's already getting a little of her color back."

As all eyes fastened on JoAnna's face, her cheeks pinkened even more.

"Well . . . okay, I guess." Bob gave in unwillingly, his keen gaze still on his sister's flushed face.

Luke rose to his full height. None of her family questioned his right to be there. "I think we should get them home and into bed." He spoke softly and yet at the same time as one accustomed to having his ideas obeyed.

The unspoken command worked immediately, and soon they were making their way to the cars. Peter was between Jean and Tom and JoAnna was carried by Luke with Bob following slightly behind.

When it came time to get in the cars, without a word to anyone Luke placed JoAnna in the Bronco. Again no one protested.

"See you at Peter's, Jo," Bob called before he backed his car out of its parking space. "You too, Luke."

Suddenly self-conscious of being alone with Luke, JoAnna stared out the window. She watched the scenery outside as he swung the car around to follow in Bob's wake, her eyes lingering for a moment on the Coast Guard station and on the boat that had carried them to safety. But soon they were drawn to the approaching car-laden ferry that was slowly making its way to the nearby landing, and her thoughts automatically went back to the night she and Luke had ridden on board and the heaven and hell that followed.

As the car wound through the afternoon traffic, JoAnna remained deep in her own thoughts. Only when the drive to Peter's seemed to take longer than it should did she focus her eyes on her surroundings and blink in surprise.

"We're not going to Peter's!" she accused, turning to stare at Luke.

"That's right," he agreed.

"We're almost home!"

"Right again. That's where I said you needed to be."

"But I thought . . . *everyone* thought you meant Peter's."

"Now, why would they think that? Peter's house isn't yours." A taunting smile was pulling at his firm lips.

JoAnna stared at him speechlessly. Then she flared, "You heard Bob—he said he'd see us at Peter's."

"He didn't say when."

"But they'll be worried about me!"

"No."

"What do you mean, no? Of course they'll be worried about me! They don't know you—at least, not very well."

"After last night and today they do" came the grim reply, all traces of humor leaving his face.

JoAnna could only continue to stare at him.

In a few short minutes they were pulling into the drive that led to her house. When the car stopped, JoAnna made an attempt to open the door, but much to her disgust her fingers were clumsy and fumbled with the catch.

Luke was across and had swung it open before she could make another attempt. She looked into his mocking eyes and stiffened her shoulders, the memory of how she had left him the day before rushing into her mind—the memory of him reaching out and drawing the redhead into his arms.

When he reached for her, she snapped, "I can walk! I don't need your help!"

He paid no attention, scooping her up into his arms and mounting the stairs.

By this time JoAnna's temper was beginning to make itself felt. She was tired and hungry and the way he was acting was making her decidedly cross. What right did he have to practically kidnap her from her family? They had

172

been upset enough over the past hours. They didn't need more worry! She loved Luke but he didn't know that. And when she had needed him so badly, he had remained as emotionless as a dead fish!

"Put me down, Luke!" she cried angrily as he pushed open her front door.

"I'll put you down when I'm ready."

JoAnna began to struggle but his arms only tightened, controlling her movements with ease. He didn't pause until they entered the bathroom. There he stopped and stood her on her feet.

"Get out of those damp things. I'll start the shower."

JoAnna's emerald eyes widened. "What?"

"I said get out of those things. You've been wet since yesterday afternoon."

"Well, I'm certainly not going to get undressed while you're in here!" Injured dignity caused her to ruffle.

Luke's blue-gray eyes gleamed. "Why not?"

"Because... because...." JoAnna sputtered, anger and embarrassment making her tongue twist. "Because I'm not, that's why!"

"I know what a woman looks like without her clothes."

JoAnna's temper boiled over. "I'm sure you do!" she snapped. "All types, varieties, and shades! But *I'm* not used to undressing in front of men! So get out! I'll take my damned shower, but I *won't* have an audience while I do!"

Putting that much energy into her anger was a mistake. Suddenly JoAnna's head began to swim. She reached out a hand to steady herself and much to her dismay found that what she encountered was Luke's hard chest. Startled, she looked up.

His pale eyes bored into her own. "There are times, JoAnna Davis, when I could strangle you cheerfully." His voice was filled with suppressed emotion. "I'm not planning a great seduction scene! All I'm trying to do is help you!"

JoAnna's heart was beating faster. "I don't need that kind of help!"

"The hell you don't! Look at you. You can hardly stand!"

"Then I'll *crawl* in!"

Luke muttered an imprecation under his breath. "All right! Have it your way! But if you're not out of here in ten minutes, I'm coming in to get you. You're stubborn enough to drown yourself rather than ask for my help!"

JoAnna said nothing as he pushed his way past and closed the door.

The shower was wonderful—washing away the damp, sticky feeling, cleaning the salt out of her hair and off her skin, warming her. Soon she lost all track of time. It was only Luke's voice calling from the other side of the shower curtain that reminded her of her limit.

"Are you still alive?" His tone was ironic.

"Of course," JoAnna answered quickly, realizing that at any moment he could put his head around the curtain. She tried desperately to cover herself, but all that was available was a totally inadequate washcloth. But Luke made no move to push aside the curtain. Instead he murmured, "Your ten minutes are up and the soup's hot. Don't be much longer."

"I—I won't," JoAnna assured him in a wavery voice.

She heard him move away and the door shut. With flying fingers she finished soaping her body and rinsed off, knowing that next time she might not be so lucky.

After toweling herself dry she dressed in the short terry wrapper she used as a bathrobe and dried her hair as best she could with another towel, the curls automatically falling into some semblance of order. Once that was done, she opened the door and peeped outside. A major disadvantage of her house was that the bathroom opened onto the hall that opened onto the living room. Anyone in the living room would have a perfect view of someone coming out of the bathroom and vice versa. That was what happened now. Luke was standing beside the table, ladling soup into a bowl. He glanced around and saw her at the same moment as she opened the door. JoAnna frowned in irritation. She had entertained visions of hurrying to her room to change, but from the determined look on Luke's face, he was going to insist that she eat first.

As the delicious smell of chicken soup met her nostrils, she decided that he was right. Her attire was a little unconventional, but if she tied the belt securely, it would do. The wrapper's hem hit her mid-thigh, so it really gave her more coverage than her shorts. But as she decided this and moved forward, something about Luke's wholly masculine appraisal made her pause. Once she had read that a little covering was more tantalizing than total nudity—and from the appreciative gleam in Luke's eye, it seemed the article was right.

JoAnna swallowed nervously, feeling about fifteen. Most women at twenty-five would know how to carry this off—but she didn't. An arrested case of virginity, that was what she was.

"It's going to get cold if you stand there much longer."

She started as Luke's sardonic voice broke into her thoughts.

"Oh!" Feeling extremely self-conscious, she moved to take a seat. "Aren't you having any?" she asked, more to have something to say than really caring.

"Not now." He took a seat across from her.

JoAnna tried to concentrate on her food, but since his eyes roamed over her face and down the vee of exposed skin that led to her breasts, she had an extremely difficult time. After several long moments under that devastating inspection, her fingers began to tremble so badly that she was forced to lay the spoon on the table, her bowl still half full.

"Finish it," she was ordered.

"I—I can't. . . ."

"Surely you're hungrier than that! Try to eat a little more. Soup isn't that filling."

"I don't want any more, really. I think I'm more tired than anything else." She tried to fake a yawn but instantly it turned into the real thing.

"Okay, you're probably right." He scooted his chair back. "Come on, I'll tuck you in."

"You don't have to do that!" JoAnna protested, panic beginning to build. "I can manage on my own." She didn't want him to put her into bed!

"No, I don't think so. Anyway, I promised your sister-in-law that I'd look after you."

"Jean?" JoAnna asked blankly.

Luke nodded.

"Jean knew about this?"

Again he nodded, his eyes narrowing as a fine tension seemed to build within him.

"But . . . why?"

"I told her we were getting married."

A roaring started in JoAnna's ears and her heart began thumping so hard she thought it was going to leap out.

"Why would you do a thing like that?" she whispered, hardly believing that she had heard right. Yet with Luke standing there so calmly and his voice being so firm, she knew she had to believe it.

"Because we are."

"But I thought you never wanted to get married!" That protest was all she could think of.

"People change."

"But . . . why me? I thought—"

Luke bent down and pulled her unresisting body from the chair, his hands fixed on her upper arms, dragging her up against him. "Because you've almost driven me out of my mind, that's why!" he stated roughly.

For a proposal it left a lot to be desired. He looked as if he would rather shred her than ravish her.

"But, Luke—"

"Do you know how I found out about you yesterday, JoAnna?" He bit out the words, anger suddenly vibrating from his powerful form. JoAnna shook her head dazedly. "I had to break the damn lock on your door because the telephone was ringing off the wall. I didn't know you were gone so when you didn't answer it, I was afraid that something had happened to you. Especially after the way I had used my friend's sister to make you jealous. As it was, I was right. But I didn't have the exact location. You were off floating somewhere in the middle of the damned Gulf of Mexico. You could have been killed!"

JoAnna didn't know what to say and she couldn't drag her eyes away from the harsh expression in his. Finally she managed a defensive, "We weren't that far out."

"Hell, I don't care how far out you were—you were far enough! Think how I felt when your sister-in-law asked if you were here. She had hoped the two of you were sheltering from the storm. The Coast Guard had checked everywhere else they thought you might be."

He shook her slightly but instead of frightening her, a strange sense of wonder descended on JoAnna's slender body. For all at once she realized that Luke must love her. He wouldn't be acting this way if he didn't. He might not have admitted it, but for a man such as he to even speak of marriage meant more than it did for most men.

"Why do you want to marry me, Luke?" she whispered.

He stared hard at her for a moment before thrusting her away and pacing over to the window that overlooked the water. JoAnna had to sink back into her chair. Being cast adrift in a storm was nothing to the experience she was going through now!

"Why?" she persisted when he seemed unwilling to go on.

When he did speak, the words seemed to be torn from him. "Because I want you! Because when I thought you might not be found, I wanted—I wanted to go off somewhere and— Dammit, Jo!"

He was across the room and had gathered her into his arms before she could draw another breath. His eyes were tortured as he looked down into her face. Then his mouth was on hers, kissing her fiercely, hungrily. With a murmur of delight, JoAnna arched her body closer to his, melting against him.

"I want you!" he rasped, the words barely above a whisper yet with the intensity not lessened by their quietness.

JoAnna didn't protest as he swept her fully into his arms and strode across the floor to her bedroom. There he placed her gently on the bed and with slow deliberation untied the knot that was the only hindrance to his full enjoyment of her body.

JoAnna closed her eyes as a wave of sweet pleasure

washed over her. She heard his rough intake of breath as the folds of her bathrobe parted, then the soft rustling of clothing as he quickly removed his own garments.

The first touch of his warm, hard body on hers reverberated through JoAnna like an electric shock and she wanted to cry out in joyful appreciation. He hadn't said it yet, but he loved her! He wanted to marry her—and that was all that mattered.

His hands stroked the smooth curves of her body, lingering on the rounded peaks of her breasts before moving to cover her flat stomach and on below where no man had ever touched. He buried his lips at her throat, a burning trail of sensation on her tender skin.

JoAnna's breathing was short, almost nonexistent. She was afraid the magic would end if she did anything to pierce the bubble. But soon a rising tide of intense excitement welled up within her and, lost to the feeling, she cried out his name in aching need.

Luke raised his head, his pale eyes glazed with desire as they locked with her own. Then the searing fire of his mouth was on hers, parting her lips with demanding urgency.

But JoAnna was inexperienced. She had never gone this far before. Instinctively she tried to protect herself when he demanded yet more intimacies.

"Let me touch you, Jo—let me touch you. My God, don't stop me now!"

JoAnna responded to the aching desire of his voice. She opened like a flower at the first kiss of spring.

Soon Luke was moving above her, nudging her legs farther apart with his own. When she felt the first thrust of his male hardness, she was aware of a sudden rigidity that tautened the powerful muscles of his back. But it was too late—Luke could hold back no longer.

JoAnna experienced a stinging pain and then esctasy. She was caught in the whirlpool of their mutual passion and rode it, until with shuddering release they once again became aware of time and place.

Luke was lying on his back, his hands folded under his dark head, his eyes fixed on the ceiling. "Why didn't you tell me?" he asked, his voice curiously devoid of emotion.

JoAnna lay beside him, trying to pull the tangled mess of her terry robe over her naked body.

"What?" she whispered, wanting him to hold her, to tell her that he loved only her. Instead she was getting nothing —nothing except an arctic coolness.

"That you were a virgin."

"I—I thought I had."

He absorbed her words for a moment. "Maybe you did. But I didn't believe you."

JoAnna sat up, partially securing the robe about her, her heart feeling like a lead weight. It all came back to the same thing. He had thought she was experienced and she wasn't—at least not until a few minutes ago. And he liked his women . . . sophisticated. Inexperience probably bored him. She swallowed tightly on the lump in her throat and murmured huskily, "I'll go get dressed."

Luke jackknifed into a sitting position and his hand shot out to grasp her wrist. "No!"

JoAnna's mouth began to tremble slightly. She didn't know what to say, what to do. She was one huge ball of misery. She should have known better than to let things get so far out of control. Luke didn't love her. She had read something into his words that was not there. And right now he was probably regretting that he had ever mentioned marriage. Or had he done that simply to get what he wanted from her? If so, he had succeeded marvelously well!

An unreadable expression passed over Luke's hard features as he saw the tears that formed in JoAnna's eyes. Slowly he released his grip on her wrist.

Even in her despair, JoAnna was very much aware of Luke's nudity as he sat beside her; and sensing this, he dragged the edge of the light coverlet up over his hips. JoAnna closed her eyes as if in pain.

"We need to talk, Jo," he stated thinly.

JoAnna shrugged her shoulders helplessly.

"When will you marry me?" The words startled her by their unexpectedness.

"You don't have to do that, Luke," she answered tightly. "I knew what I was doing."

"I asked, when will you marry me?" The stubborn question came again.

"And I said you don't have to! I'm a big girl. I know the way things are." JoAnna's green eyes flashed, hurt and determination reflected in their depths.

Luke's mouth thinned into a straight line. "I'm asking because I *want* to marry you. For no other reason."

"But wanting isn't enough, Luke, not for me!" The cry came from her soul.

Luke watched her for several long moments before he sighed deeply and said, "I've had a lot of wrong ideas about you from the beginning, Jo. I guess you could say that we got off to a bad start." He gave a short, unamused laugh and ran his fingers through his hair in a disturbed motion. "All along you were an irritant to me. I wanted to come down here, fix up the place I bought, and then rest. I didn't want to get involved with a female. But there you were. The proverbial thorn in my side. No matter how hard I tried not to think of you, I did. In fact, the harder I tried, the more I thought of you. It was something like telling a child repeatedly not to do something—they become obsessed with doing it.

"Then when I was hurt, everything changed. Suddenly it hit me that you were more important to me than just another conquest . . . and I also came to the conclusion that that boyfriend of yours was exaggerating. I thought that you might have been around, but not nearly as much as he was saying. Then . . . well, then I got scared."

He looked sideways at JoAnna, a muscle twitching in his strong jaw. "I've never allowed myself to get close emotionally to any woman and there I found myself wanting to protect you. It was a pretty unsettling experience. I had to have time to think. But I didn't want to lose contact with you. So I decided that if we started over . . . took things slow. . . . Then everything started going wrong. I lost my temper and said some things—did some things—things that came back to haunt me."

JoAnna was very still.

Luke took another deep breath before he continued. "I know what you want me to say. You want me to tell you that I love you. But I can't!" He stopped, his large hands coming out to turn her to face him fully. "I can't, Jo," he repeated. "I know that I don't want to live without you! I can tell you that much. When I thought you might be dead—" A shadow of remembered anguish crossed his rugged features. "I've never felt for a woman what I feel for you! Call it love if you want, I don't know. . . ."

A flicker of dawning hope began to sing in JoAnna's soul and a tremulous smile, filled with only a portion of her love for this man, began to curve her lips as she asked softly, "And that's why you want to marry me?"

"Yes." Luke held her tender gaze.

"Then I agree."

Luke remained motionless, as if stunned.

JoAnna's smile strengthened. "I'll call it love, Luke, because that's the way I feel and I *know* that I love you."

Luke's grip tightened convulsively on her shoulders and she knew that she was seeing a side of him that not many people were ever privileged to witness. Everyone had insecurities—fears—even the most brave. But bravery was the facing of those fears, and with her help, maybe one day he would come to recognize his true feelings for her. For now she was satisfied.

She had once wondered about the scars his early life had inflicted upon him, wondered if they still hurt. And all along they had been evident. But never more so than now. He was afraid to let himself love, afraid to put all his emotional trust in one person for fear that he would be hurt once again.

JoAnna raised her free hand and gently touched his tanned cheek. "I love you, Luke. I've loved you for a very long time."

His gray-blue eyes burned into her own but all too soon a dullness seemed to overshadow their brilliance.

"Earlier, Jo," he began.

"Never mind earlier," she whispered, "unless you regret it."

"The only thing I regret," he answered huskily, "is not being as gentle with you as I could have been. I'll always regret that."

"You were gentle, Luke."

"I didn't know. . . ."

"I know."

Even at the most important time in a woman's life, nature sometimes refuses to be denied, and a huge yawn took JoAnna unawares. Almost before she had finished, Luke was lowering her back against the coverlet.

"Sleep for you now, I think," he said in amusement. "You've earned your rest today."

JoAnna kept her arms firmly clasped around his neck when he tried to straighten.

"Stay with me, Luke." She smiled at him sleepily, unwilling to let him leave.

"You look like a small, contented kitten," he teased.

"I'll be even more content if you stay with me," she tempted softly.

Luke groaned. "You may not *get* any sleep if I stay!"

JoAnna shrugged her slender shoulders. "So who needs sleep?"

Luke's rugged features softened into a smile as he looked down at her. "You do! But I'll stay. I can't resist you."

JoAnna turned happily toward him as he lowered his head to the pillow beside her own. When he gathered her into his arms, she rested her cheek on the hard muscles of his chest and let her lips touch the warm skin of his throat as the rest of her body curled against the nearness of his. Almost instantly she fell asleep, the past two days too event-filled with too little time for rest.

When Luke heard the even sound of her breathing, he gazed down at her, a tender smile on his firm mouth. Then, sighing, he moved the pillow to a more comfortable position under his head and gently kissed the soft, clean-smelling blond curls that tickled the underside of his chin.

* * *

When the first rays of morning sun filtered through the curtains of the bedroom, JoAnna slowly awakened from a deep, restful sleep only to feel the presence of a weight resting heavily across her stomach, effectively pinning her body to the bed. At first she almost panicked—she didn't know where she was, who she was with—then all at once she remembered and her emerald eyes turned to feast themselves on Luke's still-sleeping form.

She could scarcely believe that what had happened was true. And yet, here he was, in her bed, lying beside her, an arm possessively clasping her to him as if he was concerned that she might try to slip away.

Tenderly JoAnna allowed her eyes to dwell on each dearly loved plane and hollow of his face, on the dark, spiky lashes that crescented each cheek, on the strong, straight nose that could be termed a little large, on the shadow of bristle where his beard had grown overnight. . . .

Unable to resist, JoAnna slowly leaned forward and kissed the relaxed line of his mouth that even in sleep was sensuously disturbing. Her touch was that of a butterfly, soft and sweet. When Luke did not awaken, she leaned forward again, strengthening the pressure and letting it linger.

Still Luke showed no sign of consciousness, and with a soft giggle JoAnna tried again. Only this time, when she leaned forward to touch his lips, he shifted position without warning and crushed her to the bed, his mouth taking passionate possession of her own.

"Is that the way you plan to wake me every morning when we're married?" he questioned huskily, when at last he ended the kiss.

JoAnna smiled lovingly into the warmth of his eyes. "Of course," she promised.

"Then I think our marriage might work."

JoAnna twined her arms about the strong column of his neck, enjoying the feel of his powerful body against her own. She trailed her fingers through the dark thickness of his hair and breathed, "I still can't believe this is true. Are you real, Luke, or am I dreaming?"

Luke stroked the curve of her breast that her loosened robe revealed, allowing one finger to tease the hardening peak. "If you're dreaming, then so am I and I'll kill anyone who wakes us!"

JoAnna's hand slowly fell away from his hair as a serious expression clouded her green eyes. "Luke, you don't have to marry me. If you want, I'll just stay with you." Her heart was trip-hammering in her breast but she meant every word. If Luke preferred to ignore the legal ceremony, she was willing to also. She loved him and she knew that he loved her—even if he couldn't tell her so yet. And if he needed the feeling of freedom. . . .

Luke stared down at her, the hand on her breast motionless. Finally he spoke, saying quietly, "Some of the marriages I've seen haven't been very good examples, but for us I won't have it any other way. I asked you to marry me, Jo. Not live with me."

"But I don't mind," she protested.

"*I* do." Smoky gray-blue eyes held hers steadily.

Almost in slow motion, JoAnna reached out to touch the bronzed skin of his cheek. She touched it wondrously, reverently. "I love you, Luke," she whispered.

Luke turned his face until his lips were touching her palm. "Will you marry me today?" he asked.

Startled by the suddenness, JoAnna echoed, "Today?"

Luke smiled. "Why not? We can have the rest of the week for a honeymoon."

JoAnna blinked. "But what about my job?"

"What about it?"

"Mr. Daniels . . . Melissa . . . they need me!"

Luke shifted to lie on his back, his hands folded under his head. "They can get along without you for a while longer. When Jean called yesterday to tell them you had been found, your boss was so relieved he told her to tell you not to come back for the rest of the week—to take time to recuperate."

JoAnna digested this piece of information. For Mr. Daniels to say that! But then maybe he had finally found out what an excellent secretary Melissa was. And anyway, she thought, if I marry Luke. . . . JoAnna raised up to prop her blond curls on the heel of her hand.

"Luke? Where will we live? In Houston?"

Luke turned to look at her, his pale eyes running down over the expanse of velvety skin her parted robe exposed before coming to rest on her face. "Would you mind very much if we do? We could always keep the beach houses— one for us, one for the kids."

"*Kids?*"

"Sure."

JoAnna took a deep breath. "Don't you think you're planning things a bit too . . . quickly?"

"Don't you want children?"

The thought of a child as a product of their love thrilled her, but she wanted Luke to herself for a while. She wanted to come to know him completely—to have him trust her completely.

"Well . . . yes . . . eventually," she stammered.

"So do I . . . eventually." Luke gathered her to him. "If

we haven't already started one," he whispered close to her ear.

JoAnna's green eyes widened. "That's true," she agreed slowly, revising the plans she had made. A child in nine months would be wonderful. And they would have all the time before to devote to each other, not to mention a ready-made playmate in Tom and Sally's baby.

Luke laughed softly at the play of thoughts that could be read easily on her oval face. "So you'll marry me today," he stated teasingly.

JoAnna lifted her chin with pretended haughtiness, now realizing the game he was playing. "Of course," she replied. "It would only be proper."

"To give the 'maybe' baby a name."

JoAnna nodded, the twinkle in her eyes growing to match his. "Try to stop me," she murmured.

"Well, in that case, since you agree—" Luke began to slip the robe from her shoulders. "And since the march might already be stolen—" He threw the offending robe to the floor. "I don't see why we can't—"

He never finished the sentence. JoAnna stopped him with her lips, and soon the quickened fires of their mutual need fulfilled the promise of his unspoken words.

LOOK FOR NEXT MONTH'S
CANDLELIGHT ECSTASY ROMANCES™

42 THE ARDENT PROTECTOR, *Bonnie Drake*
43 A DREAM COME TRUE, *Elaine Raco Chase*
44 NEVER AS STRANGERS, *Suzanne Simmons*
45 RELENTLESS ADVERSARY, *Jayne Castle*
46 RESTORING LOVE, *Suzanne Sherill*
47 DAWNING OF DESIRE, *Susan Chatfield*

Love—the way you want it!

Candlelight Romances

			TITLE NO.	
☐ LOVE'S BRIGHTEST HOUR by Elaine Smith	$1.75	#688	(18530-0)
☐ A VINTAGE YEAR by Jessica Elliot	$1.75	#689	(19383-4)
☐ BOLD VENTURE by Coleen Moore	$1.75	#690	(10517-X)
☐ A MERRY CHASE by Rebecca Bennet	$1.75	#691	(15596-7)
☐ A SUITABLE MARRIAGE by Marlaine Kyle	$1.75	#692	(18406-1)
☐ WELL MET BY MOONLIGHT by Rowena Wilson	$1.75	#683	(19553-5)
☐ SPLENDOR BY THE SEA by Darla Benton	$1.75	#684	(17257-8)
☐ SUSIE by Jennie Tremaine	$1.75	#685	(18391-X)
☐ THE INNOCENT ADULTERESS by Dee Stuart	$1.75	#686	(14045-5)
☐ LADY NELL by Sandra Mireles	$1.75	#687	(14675-5)
☐ THE IMPOSSIBLE DREAM by Dorothy Dowdell	$1.75	#672	(14177-X)
☐ IN THE NAME OF LOVE by Arlene Hale	$1.75	#676	(14724-7)
☐ MISS CLARINGDON'S CONDITION by Laureen Kwock	$1.75	#680	(11467-5)
☐ THE IMPOVERISHED HEIRESS by Diana Burke	$1.75	#681	(13842-6)
☐ THE UNSUITABLE LOVERS by Phoebe Matthews	$1.75	#682	(14953-3)
☐ WHISPERS OF LOVE by Barbara Max	$1.50	#673	(19523-3)
☐ THE INDIFFERENT HEART by Alexandra Sellers	$1.50	#674	(14150-8)
☐ LOVE PLAYS A PART by Nina Pykare	$1.50	#675	(14725-5)

At your local bookstore or use this handy coupon for ordering:

Dell DELL BOOKS
P.O. BOX 1000, PINEBROOK, N.J. 07058-1000

Please send me the above title. I am enclosing $ _____
(please add 75¢ per copy to cover postage and handling). Send check or money order—no cash or C.O.D.'s. Please allow up to 8 weeks for shipment.

Mr/Mrs/Miss _____

Address _____

City _____ State/Zip _____

VOLUME I IN THE EPIC NEW SERIES

The Morland Dynasty

The Founding

by Cynthia Harrod-Eagles

THE FOUNDING, a panoramic saga rich with passion and excitement, launches Dell's most ambitious series to date—THE MORLAND DYNASTY.

From the Wars of the Roses and Tudor England to World War II, THE MORLAND DYNASTY traces the lives, loves and fortunes of a great English family.

A DELL BOOK $3.50   #12677-0

At your local bookstore or use this handy coupon for ordering:

	THE FOUNDING $3.50 #12677-0
Dell	**DELL BOOKS** P.O. BOX 1000, PINE BROOK, N.J. 07058-1000

Please send me the above title. I am enclosing $_____$ (please add 75¢ per copy to cover postage and handling). Send check or money order—no cash or C.O.D.'s. Please allow up to 8 weeks for shipment.

Mr./Mrs./Miss_____

Address_____

City_____State/Zip_____

Danielle Steel

AMERICA'S LEADING LADY OF ROMANCE REIGNS OVER ANOTHER BESTSELLER

A Perfect Stranger

A flawless mix of glamour and love by Danielle Steel, the bestselling author of *The Ring, Palomino* and *Loving*.

A DELL BOOK $3.50   #17221-7

At your local bookstore or use this handy coupon for ordering:

Dell | DELL BOOKS   A PERFECT STRANGER $3.50   #17221-7
P.O. BOX 1000, PINE BROOK, N.J. 07058-1000

Please send me the above title. I am enclosing $_____ (please add 75¢ per copy to cover postage and handling). Send check or money order—no cash or C.O.D.'s. Please allow up to 8 weeks for shipment.

Mr./Mrs./Miss _____

Address _____

City _____ State/Zip _____